The 80's Story

THE STRUGGLES OF THE AFRICAN AMERICAN MIND POST CIVIL RIGHTS MOVEMENT

Professor Mustaafa

authorHOUSE®

AuthorHouse™
1663 Liberty Drive
Bloomington, IN 47403
www.authorhouse.com
Phone: 1-800-839-8640

First published by AuthorHouse   08/15/2011

ISBN: 978-1-4567-5509-6 (sc)
ISBN: 978-1-4567-5508-9 (ebk)

INTRODUCTION

What do you do when you love someone but at the time era that you live in doesn't accept you loving that person? How would you feel to have nobody support you in that quest for happiness even though the life you choose to live is a good one. People often can't put there differences aside and they think that the control they try to have over somebody that they care about will be good for them but in reality they are pushing them away. How would you feel if the decisions that you make in your life could affect your children with you not even knowing, would you change your choices?

We try to justify our actions by saying were doing it for other people. We might believe at the time but it's really not the case and due to blindness we forget about the fact that we can't control anybody. Weather it be a man trying to control a woman or vice versa or a parent trying to control a kid. Have you ever looked into somebody's eyes and seen them give you a look back as if they're crying out "let me live my life?" If you have, did you actually think about giving them that courtesy?

The Eighties Story is based on the drug game and a war between two families, an African American and Italian American family that spills over into a following generations. It deals with loyalty and betrayal, love, trust, control, lust and hate. The Cartone family is the mob of Southern California and the daughter of the mob boss Gina is married to an African American doctor named Jimmy. Jimmy's brother Tony happens to be an up and coming drug kingpin who wants Paul Cartone's spot in the drug game. Jimmy and Gina try to prevent altercations between their families but are not successful when Tony decides to murder one of Gina's brothers.

The Cartone family is also at war with the other Mob family in California name the Delena family who wants to run the Cartones out of the drug business due to jealousy that Carlo Delena has for Paul Cartone and his ambition to be the only mob boss in California. On the flip side Tony is also dealing with various men in his neighborhood that want his spot and will do anything to get it include conspire with the Cartone family to take him out.

The feud doesn't die down between the two families, but instead gets worse when the participants children happen to rekindle the feud years later. Terell, Tony's son takes over his father's business in the eighties and Henry Cartone the grandson of Paul Cartone also joins in the feud. Brian isn't Tony's son by blood but Tony took him in at ten years old. His best friend Marvin is actually his father. After a cold incident between the two men that involves Marvin's death, Tony takes Brian in and Brian refers to Tony as his father. When he returns he is eighteen and moves back to stay with Tony. Things have changed but his mind state to be out of the family business is in tact, he falls in love with Elana who is Jimmy and Gina's daughter which further complicates matters. This story is about a lot more than drugs and racism. Also in the mix is Giovanni who is Elana's brother, he is on the side with Henry Cartone going against his own family to and he has an important choice to make.

———

The Eighties story symbolizes the first phase of African American life post civil rights movement. It was the time when we were lost as a race. After Malcolm X, Martin Luther King, and the Panthers were gone black people lost a lot of fight. The first phase of our self-destruction has been drugs. Weather it was selling or using it was killing us off and that's what this story represents. Like this story some blacks didn't fall in the trap, but a lot did. I'm not trying to give all the answers I want to sum up my heritage in three parts from what I've heard about how we lived as a whole. This is the first installment and be ready to read a story about a young man's courage, two families torn, the struggles of mixed children, loyalty and betrayal and much more.

The year is 1963, Jimmy Taylor and his new wife Gina Taylor walked along a pier in Los Angeles California, enjoying the feeling of being one collective soul in the eyes of God. The sky was dark and it had a romantic vibe all around. Love was a blossomed airborne emotion that settled in the depths of the two souls. The pier was holding them up physically but the scenery around them was holding them up in a spiritual and emotional way. To them it was nobody else that existed in the world and for the next couple of days that bliss would be at its peak.

It was a small wedding with only three participants, the two of them and a priest. The reason for the threesome wedding was because none of their family agreed with the relationship, let alone a marriage. Jimmy was an African American male and Gina was an Italian American woman and in the time that the two lovers lived in that was not accepted on either side. Besides the race issue, there was a war brooding within the two families. Gina's father Paul Cartone was running the drug game in Southern California also there was Jimmy's brother Tony who was an up and coming drug Kingpin who wanted Cartone's spot in the drug game.

Jimmy wasn't involved in any criminal activity. He was a hard working doctor and one of the few black doctors in the city. His reputation was impeccable he had what they called the healing hand. He was loved all around the community, besides a couple of die hard community members who were against inter-racial relationships. His precision with any sharp object in surgery was crisp, and his brain was like a sponge when it came to anything medical. He even had a tight grasp on mental illness which was something that wasn't known too well back in the sixties. Jimmy was a tall and handsome brown skinned man. He had broad shoulders and a young looking face. His eyes talked to you so loud that when he spoke you would barely acknowledge that fact that his lips were moving because his pupils kept you mesmerized.

Gina was the perfect housewife and that's all she wanted to do because those small duties kept her content which was the kind of woman that Jimmy wanted. They complimented each other and she a had a great way of easing his mind after a long day. They did a lot together whenever they had the time and she understood the kind of work that he did was important so she didn't complain about the amount of time he spent helping people.

Gina knew about her family business and tried her best to stay away from it. Both of them acknowledged the war between their families brewing, yet neither cared, they loved they're families but they loved each other deeper. Gina was curvaceous with olive oil skin and long hair that came down to her back. She had full lips, and brown eyes, the dimples in her cheeks went extremely deep when she smiled which made her stand out. Her cheekbones weren't too high and her exotic look attracted men.

As they walked along the pier they expressed to each other their dreams about the life they've shared along with the lives they created with they're children and the life they vowed to make a happy one.

"What religion do you want our children to be?" Gina asked.

"Baptist or Catholic, it doesn't matter to me, as long as they love God I'm going to be a happy man." Jimmy responded with a smile on his face. He didn't see religion as some kind of colt where you had to engage in it with a certain way or style of practice.

"Are you sure Tony doesn't mind watching them while were on our honeymoon?" Gina asked. She trusted Tony with her children because those were his niece and nephew, but as a new mother her instinct kicked in automatically.

"Of course, he has Terrell and Marvin's kid is over there with him all the time, so he's happy to do this for us." Jimmy said attempting to ease his wife's mind.

A smell of trouble started to infest the clean air they breathed. An eerie vibe came along with it and made Jimmy tense up. Gina was caught up in the love for her husband to even think about the feeling Jimmy sensed. He ignored his feelings and kept in stride with his wife.

A black Cadillac came to a screeching halt in front of them which confirmed Jimmy's suspicion of trouble ahead. Gina froze up and her ecstatic mind state froze along with her body. Her eldest brother and air to the family business Mario hopped out of the car faster than lightning striking. His fat belly jiggled because of the urgency he showed extending his body out the restrictions of his car door that he could barely fit threw. He was a short man with thick sideburns and no other facial hair. His hat sat on his head tightly, and his suit looked too small. He looked like a full fledged mobster and his demeanor would frighten some of the most hardened criminals.

Mario wobbled over to the couple with a gun in his hand anticipating the confrontation with Jimmy. His family with the exception of Gina and the youngest son of Paul Cartone Vincent despised the fact that any member of their family would get so close to a black person, even one with the upmost respect for the law. His palm was trembling but not because of fear, it was because he knew if Jimmy said or did anything that was slightly disrespectful he would pump him full of lead. Once he got in front of the two he stared Jimmy down with a wild look in his eyes then shortly turned his attention to his sister.

Mario's presence ruined the beauty of the atmosphere that the two created. His angry vibe overshadowed the love built by the aftermath of a beautiful wedding ceremony. Every step he took seemed like it would split the sky in half and chase off the stars that glimmered in the night time. His heavy foot symbolized a ton of weight cracking down the golden cement that formed on the pier that they glided on.

"Gina, why are still with this nigger? Pop isn't mad about the kids anymore, even though they're half nigger, they still have our family blood. Come on home and leave this nigger to himself." Mario was pleading with his sister at this point. He recalled the argument his father had with her about her children.

When she first found out that she was pregnant Paul had dismissed the children and told Gina that he would spit in their face before he accepted them as Cartones. After he said that she made it up in her mind that she would keep them away from her father forever. Jimmy being naive felt that people could change and asked her not to be so solid in her position but he supported any decision she made concerning her family's contact with their kids.

"No Mario! I won't be around you until you guys and papa accept my husband!" As she made her point she locked arms with Jimmy showing her brother their solidarity. Mario's facial expression went from apologetic to enraged he glared at Jimmy but still spoke to his sister.

"No Gina, don't tell me you married this nigger!" Mario hollered.

"If another nigger comes from your lips I swear it will be your last word." Jimmy calmly stated. He had enough of her family, it had been years since Gina and Jimmy found love and been together. He knew the times he lived in, he wasn't some silly idealist that believed and sung we shall overcome songs but he had enough of Mario's taunting. He knew Mario could easily kill him but at this point he made a rare dumb decision not to care about his life and it was due to the extreme amount of disrespect that Mario was showing him.

"Oh, he has some balls after all, come on Jimmy just try something." Mario spewed as he raised the gun in his hands directly at Jimmy's face.

Gina knew Mario wouldn't shoot her so she quickly stepped in front of Jimmy to give him a shield. Mario stared at his sister like he had no idea who she was. She picked some black man over her own family. She listened to the Supremes and Temptations, admired the African American culture which came across to her family as they're culture and lifestyle wasn't good enough for her. He felt his sister slipping over to the dark side so to speak. Mario was speechless so he shot Jimmy one last glare and then turned around and walked back to his car. He sat in the driver seat and turned the car on. Frank Sinatra's voice came out of the radio as he drove off in a rage. He didn't expect to hear that Gina had married Jimmy but that's the decision that Gina made and even though he felt she spat in his face he wouldn't harm his sister. But Jimmy on the other hand, Mario was hoping to find a reason to kill him. His father wouldn't okay it unless he had a reason to but according to Mario being black and having his hands on his sister was enough to kill him.

The year was 1973 and Tony sat in the bar in his house which also had a pool table and three lounge couches on each sides of the room except for the side where the bar was located. He had pictures of Malcolm X and the Black Panthers holding guns all across his walls. He had a couple of small tables around the bar. He also had four stools in front of the bar and one behind the bar where he was seated. He had a television set on the wall by the entrance from the living room that set in a marble entertainment system. The floors were marble and there was a sliding glass door that led into the backyard.

The living room was like a large private study with candles, burning incents, and a record player. The couches were suede and it had a tan carpet along with a tan coat of paint on the wall. He had different old newspapers like the various Panther papers and Muhammad Speaks lying on a coffee table in front of his couch and loveseat.

His home wasn't your typical millionaire home it was humble and low-key like he was. It was brick and wood on the outside, a small cozy abode with a large yard around it. Tony didn't have animals because they were too messy, and he felt they should be in the wild. In his mind they were survivalist just like black people no matter how big or small they were.

Tony wasn't just a drug dealer he was also an activist who believed in the "By any means necessary" philosophy. He had no respect for the law, he had killed a couple cops and never got caught because of his brain and the way he maneuvered. He was just as smart as his brother Jimmy but in a more ruthless street sense. He was in the middle of his drink when he had company pop his head through the front entrance of his bar.

Larry came in and placed himself on one of the stools in front of the bar. He was sickly skinny with a large head. Every feature he had on his face was large and he was quite ugly. Larry had convinced himself that he was going to leave the powder alone and start to sell it. He didn't want to be a nickel and dime cat so he figured the way to get in the game was to talk to the Kingpin. Tony knew Larry for years, they were never close but they used to hang out together back when Tony first got into crime.

Larry had an act for trying to get over on anybody and he didn't have a loyal bone in his body. The way Tony saw it Larry would either snort all his product up which would be bad for business and he would have to come looking for him. The other outcome would be that Larry could actually be successful but would become a risk to him, maybe not financially but as far as greed and power. The drug game is filled with ambitious men who want the top spot and Tony was one of them. Larry had the drive and possibly the potential so Tony wasn't going to give him the means either way.

"All I need is a couple of ounces on credit and I'll bring you your money back plus interest if you need it man." Larry pleaded his case in a sincere manner. He was certain that Tony would front him the coke because of how far back they went back.

Tony just shook his head with a look of pity on his face. "How can you sell when you do coke Larry, how can you make money for yourself, let alone pay me back?" Tony asked. He could sense the anger building in Larry because the conversation wasn't going the way that he wanted it to go.

"Come on man, I'm not that stupid, I need my money." Larry spat.

"I can't take that chance man." Tony said with a sound of finality in his voice which Larry picked up on. Larry felt his jaw clenching like he had those tweaks in him the way he used to have when he was on drugs. He was trying his hardest to watch his mouth because he saw the Dessert Eagle sitting right in front of Tony.

"You ain't a down cat man, talkin' that jive. I'm gonna get on and when I'm your new competition you gonna wish you put me on. You better watch your back man because you ain't the only one that got the heart to run these Cali streets." Larry was standing up and walking out of the bar as he spoke. As soon as he finished what he was saying Jimmy walked into the bar and sat down in the same stool that Larry was sitting in.

Jimmy was tired from a long eighteen hour shift at the hospital. Tony didn't have the kids the whole time but he watched them for some hours while Gina ran errands. Jimmy ran his hands over his face like they had some water on them and was waking him up a bit.

"What was all that about?" Jimmy asked Tony with a look of concern on his face. He knew Larry from back in the day but never trusted him so when he heard him raising his voice he automatically got worried that a problem could be in the making.

"He just blowing smoke out his ass because he can't get his life together. You're kids are safe outside in the back with the other kids. I don't treat them differently because they're half white."

Tony said with a smile on his face. He always gave Jimmy some jokes about the other half of his niece and nephew.

"When are you going to get over the fact that I sleep with an Italian woman and eat Italian food half of the week?" Jimmy asked.

"You eat ribs and chicken just like the rest of us." Tony responded. "And I told you that fact that she's white doesn't bother me, but you know what does bother me Jimmy?" Tony asked.

"She's the daughter of Paul Cartone, I know." Jimmy said finishing his statement in a mocking tone.

They went back and forth for a minute with verbal insults until Marvin walked in whistling the melody of "ABC" by the Jackson five. As soon as he walked into the room the mode changed. The sibling jokes stopped and instead they saw a gloomy shadow scatter on the walls. Marvin felt the shift of energy but didn't care because he had business to tend to. Tony who felt sorry for Marvin was thinking about getting him his drugs and getting him out of his house. The shameful part is that it wasn't always like that with Marvin and Tony.

Marvin was another of Tony's friends from when he was young. They were best friends both engaged in all kinds of criminal activities until Marvin went to jail for armed robbery. Marvin was a loser in every sense of the word. He couldn't work or hustle. The only thing he could half way do right was pimp and he couldn't keep his women around due to his short temper.

When he was released from jail him and Tony met best friends and got them pregnant at the same time, along with Jimmy getting Gina pregnant and having twins. The four children were all the same age. Jimmy's son and daughter were named Elana and Giovanni. Tony's son was named Terell and Marvin's son was named Brian. He tried to get himself straight from drugs on a few occasions but none were successful and a downward spiral started to form in him in every aspect of his life but being a father and boyfriend to Brian and Brenda was his worse aspect.

He would beat both of them to the point where Tony would have to beat on him. It would also be verbal abuse to where Brenda felt like she couldn't do better for herself. His problem with her was that she wouldn't sell her body for money but he still loved her. He respected her for it but he took his frustration out on her which she couldn't understand. Brian's verbal abuse wasn't anything personal it was due to his age, just a bunch of shut ups and taunting.

Marvin had no concept of working or hustling. To him anything he wanted done was supposed to be by a woman from cooking to cleaning. He even made a woman cut his meat up for him to degrade them in a subtle way. He could only keep a prostitute for a week before she would run off but he wheeled them in pretty easy because of his charm and debonair style. The way he spoke his words had melody to them. The way his arm swayed and his head bopped showed style. His goatee was perfectly cut and his dark brown skin had a pretty glaze to it. Marvin kept his appearance in check at all times.

Drugs were another aspect of his life that led him to a point where he was considered worthless. He did cocaine, heroin, marijuana and he did them a lot. He was high all the time and it turned into a daily routine to chase woman and to chase a high instead of being there for his. He saw no problem with drugs and felt if everybody did drugs the world might be a better place to live in.

Marvin took a seat next to Jimmy and tapped his hands on the bar top like he was playing a Congo drum. "What's up fellas? I know you got a little something for me Tony. I need some of that white girl and I'm not talking about your wife Jimmy." Marvin said with a huge smile on his face. Jimmy shook his head before he returned an insult to Marvin.

"I'm sorry Marvin I don't understand that drug addict humor." Jimmy said.

Just looking at Marvin made him feel nothing but pity for him and his tolerance of Marvin had got tested over the years.

Tony stood up and walked into the house shaking his head. Marvin and Jimmy sat in silence. Marvin walked around the bar and poured himself a shot of brandy. He slurped it down quickly and poured another one.

"So your turning into an alcoholic too huh?" Jimmy asked.

"Get off my back Jimmy, do I talk about you and what you do shacked up with a white broad." Marvin knew he irritated Jimmy and he enjoyed it. He was jealous of the relationship that Jimmy and Tony had. It bothered him that two people who were so opposite morally could get along so well. He looked at Jimmy as a square, a house slave. The fact that he had the audacity to not only marry a white girl but the daughter of Tony's enemy made him feel like he wasn't loyal to Tony.

"You need to worry about keeping your hands off your son when he does nothing to deserve it. You're a poor excuse for a father and it's a damn shame that Brenda hasn't came and got her baby." Jimmy said in a hateful manner. He knew how to irritate Marvin too, and he also enjoyed it.

Marvin's blood started to boil because Jimmy hit him with the truth and he hated to be called on his faults. If Jimmy was somebody else they would have been fighting in that bar. Tony walked back in the bar with some cocaine in a baggie. In the other hand he had a plate and he set both of them on the bar top. He walked back over to his seat and sat back down. He snatched the bottle of brandy from Marvin's grasp and another glass to pour himself a shot. He raised it to Jimmy as to offer him some but Jimmy waived it off. Marvin instantly gravitated over to the coke and poured it out of the bag. As he started to fix himself a line the four kids came running into the bar.

"I told yall about running in here like yall crazy!" snapped Tony. Giovanni and Elana ran to their father and gave him hugs. Jimmy embraced his children like he hadn't seen them in years.

"Are you guys ready to go?" asked Jimmy. As soon as he asked the question Elana's face instantly frowned up, she wanted to stay and play with her cousin and Brian. Giovanni on the other hand was ready to leave. Jimmy noticed the frown on his daughter's face.

"Don't worry baby, we'll come back again." Jimmy said consoling his daughter.

"Why do we have to go daddy?" Elana flashed her big green eyes and Jimmy's heart melted.

"Because it's getting late and we have to go eat dinner." Jimmy stood up and grabbed his kids by their hands. "I'll see you later bro, and Marvin do something with yourself for your son's sake man." Jimmy said in a condescending tone, but Marvin was so occupied with getting high that he didn't even hear Jimmy talking. Jimmy watched him for a second and then shook his head as he walked out of the bar area.

Tony lit a cigarette up as he watched Marvin looking like he was in too deep. He wanted to slap him repeatedly in the face until he got the message that drugs were deadly if you used them too much. Although he didn't agree with Marvin's actions he looked at it as what it was. Marvin was a grown man and he made his own choices just like everybody else in this world.

It was obvious that Marvin had it bad. His hands were shaking as he precisely fixed the line. He was flicking his nostrils with a force that could knock his nose hairs loose.

His son Brian slowly approached him, as he heard the light footsteps of his son he started to get annoyed because he knew the kid was going to talk to him which would take him away from his goal at the moment.

"Hey dad, my teacher said I did a good job at school today. She gave me a gold star for me reading." Brian said trying to get some form of approval and attention from his coked out father.

Marvin turned and shot him a cold look. "We all know your smart so shut up about it!" His response sent a sharp pain into Brian's heart, all he wanted to do was seek some love from his father, but instead he got hurtful words in a harsh tone.

"What is wrong with you?" Tony started. "Come here little man." He motioned Brian over to him. "Every time you do good in school come tell me and I'll give you 20 dollars, but I want to see one of those stars okay." Brian nodded and gave Tony a hug. He loved Tony more than his own father because Tony actually showed some sort of affection to him.

Marvin's anger started to flare as he viscously sniffed his line before grabbing Brian by his arm and dragging him away from Tony.

"Don't ever take nothing from no man, do you hear me!" Marvin exclaimed.

Brian didn't take any money from Tony but Marvin was upset about the fact that he gave Tony a hug. He didn't want the boy to feel any kind of bond weather it was physical or mental since he wasn't capable to have those bonds with his son himself. He didn't know why but that's how he was. Brian had a look of pure fear on his face. He felt his legs start to shake and his lips were quivering. His eyes started to tear up but he put up his best attempt to stop them from falling in fear of getting beat.

Marvin sensed his weakness and slapped him across his face so hard that it sent him flying halfway across the room and crashing hard to the floor. Brian urinated on himself as Terell ran over to him trying to help him up. Marvin stared his son down and Brian knew that the look meant that his father wasn't done so Brian slowly walked back over by his dad with his nose bleeding, tears streaming down his face, and his pants wet.

Tony calmly watched the situation at hand taking drags off his cigarette with a venomous look on his face. He ashed his cigarette, took another drag, cleared his throat, picked his gun off the bar top and pointed it at Marvin. Marvin felt danger and looked back at Tony, his eyes widened as he stared down the barrel of Tony's Dessert Eagle.

"That's the last time you hit that kid in front of me for no reason. If I see you do that again I swear on my life I will shoot you dead." Tony said in a murderous manner, he remembered seeing the beatings and wished he did something about it sooner. Marvin never was a good father but he was Tony's friend and he believed a man should be able to raise his kid how he saw fit, but enough was enough. It wasn't like Brian was a bad kid he was a great kid. He listened and was extremely intelligent, he wasn't a crybaby or spoiled, and he had a good heart.

Marvin fixed himself another line with Tony still pointing the gun at him, this time he did it fast. He sniffed the line then sat back in his chair. He looked back at Tony who still had the gun pointed at him.

"All right I know when I'm not wanted. Brian! Let's go now!" Marvin barked at his son, but Brian just watched him. His legs wouldn't allow him to move he heard every word Tony said and felt protected. Marvin couldn't believe what he was seeing. This was the first time any insoubornation had come out of his son and he blamed Tony for it.

"Now you want to turn my kid against me huh, Brian let's go!" Marvin said pointing his finger to the ground. Brian kept staring at him and Marvin got extremely angry. He walked over to his son and grabbed him by the neck forcing the child to leave with him. Brian tried to resist but he was no match for the strength Marvin had. Tony watched Marvin like a hawk, still smoking his cigarette, waiting to see if Marvin understood what he said to him. The more Marvin pulled Brian the more he tried to put up a fight and before Brian knew it Marvin slapped him again with the back of his hand. The force of the blow dropped him instantly busting his nose even worse. Blood was gushing out of his nose and before Brian could blink he heard three loud gunshots ring throughout the bar and he saw his father's body drop beside him lying limp.

Tony put his gun back on the bar top and took his shirt off. He rushed towards Brian and put his shirt up to Brian's nose to stop the bleeding. Terell came over to check on Brian and that's when Tony put the shirt in Terell's hand and tilted Brian's head back. Terell kept holding the shirt to Brian's nose as Tony went to the phone on his bar top. Marvin's blood gushed all over the floor and Brian just watched his father's body.

Brian's mind went blank for a second and then the gruesome scene came back into his head. He heard Tony tell somebody to come over to the house and help him clean a mess up but it was like everything was moving at warp speed.

Terell lowered the shirt from Brian's nose as it stopped leaking. Brian walked over to the body and kneeled beside it, he couldn't help but to think how weak his father looked to him.

Tony walked over to Brian and grabbed him by his shoulders. Brian continued his stare at his father's lifeless body while Tony spoke to him.

"Brian, listen to me, he deserved that. Do you understand me, that man deserved that." Tony said quietly. Brian finally broke the gaze at his dad and looked at Tony. "Don't nobody care more about you than me and your mother, I did you a favor, believe me your going to understand it when you grow up. So go upstairs with Terell and I'll take care of this, okay."

Brian nodded his head and backed away from Tony still looking at his father's corpse on the ground. The smell of death made his stomach turn as he was still in shock. Terell grabbed him by his arm and guided him out of the bar. Tony paced around and looked down at Marvin with tears in his eyes.

"Why did you make me do that?" Tony yelled at his deceased friend. His remorse started to creep into his mind and he immediately started to regret what he did. But he made the decision and he was going to stand by it.

———

Jimmy and Giovanni were sitting in their living room playing chess while Gina and Elana were in the kitchen preparing dinner. The aroma from the spaghetti filled the whole house and they were enjoying the peace and quiet. Jimmy didn't have a lot of family time or time for himself because of his demanding schedule as a doctor although he enjoyed his job he treasured the time spent with his family.

The home that they built portrayed an urban feel, mixed with a traditional Italian theme. There were numerous stands with vases on them that went through the living room and hallway which prevented the kids from fighting or running around in their living room. If any vases got broken they knew what would happen to them by the hands of their mother. Gina didn't dislike Italian music or dancing but she preferred the African American style of music and dancing. She listened to Frank Sinatra, Jerry Lewis and Elvis Presley but just preferred Ray Charles, Marvin Gaye, and Diana Ross. Jimmy didn't like the interior decorating but that was something that the woman had the right to pick out in his eyes so it didn't bother him.

Chess was a game that Jimmy loved. It wasn't like dominoes or cards, it didn't require an ounce of luck it was one hundred percent skill. The chess pieces along with the board was all glass which made it more valuable. He watched his son trying his hardest to keep up with his dad on the game and realized that his son was over analyzing his decision which is one of his own traits. Jimmy thought he would let his son wreck his mental for a few more seconds before giving him some advice.

"Jimmy, I need you to go to the store I forgot the garlic bread." Gina barked.

"Hold on honey, I'm about to show him how to get a checkmate." Jimmy responded a little irritated with his wife. He just worked a shift and picked up the kids now she wanted him to run to the store.

As Elana walked into the living room to see what her father was about to do in the game, there was three knocks at the door. She about faced her route and went to the door.

"Who is it?" Elana called out. As she heard her Uncle Mario's voice she opened the door. Mario walked in and hugged his niece. Gina had a bewildered look on her face because none of her family except for her baby brother Vincent ever stopped by her house. If they wanted to see her or the kids they would call her over. She immediately thought something was wrong so she put a top on the spaghetti sauce and walked into the living room. Mario scanned the room before he found Jimmy sitting down playing chess with Giovanni. He walked over to the table with his sister at his heels.

"Hey Giovanni, why don't you let me and your dad talk." Mario ordered as Gina quickly answered for her son who looked up at Mario like he sensed some tension.

"No, why don't we talk Mario." Gina said motioning her two fingers between the two of them indicating she was mentioning herself and him. "What is this about?" Gina asked grilling her brother with a cold stare. Jimmy decided that he should take control of the situation seeing his wife's distress.

Mario looked serious and he could tell that his demeanor meant he had something important to talk to him about.

"Gina, go get the bread so I can talk to your brother." Jimmy asked. It seemed like it was more of an order than him asking, so Gina granted him his wish without saying a word on the way out, Elana and Giovanni walked back into their rooms.

The two men sat and stared each other down. Jimmy felt like it was always some kind of test with Mario mentally. The room seemed like a war zone. Their minds went into battle mode in a metaphorical way. They were set to engage in a one on one fight of the minds. In Jimmy's mind it seemed like Mario knew his strength was his intelligence. Not in a book sense, but Jimmy was very street wise he just had a different set of morals than your average street wise male. Mario finally finished his visual intimidation tactic and began the discussion.

"Jimmy, this thing with my sister, this marriage, seems like the real deal. You and my sister are obviously meant for each other, besides Italian food my sister has no part of our culture, sort of like Marie. She's her mother's child, you know that right?" Jimmy's mind was trying to decipher what Mario was getting at, but he was thrown for a loop. "But Giovanni isn't, that kid is definitely more Italian than black, I'll tell ya." Mario chuckled. His chuckle made Mario's insinuation click into Jimmy's brain.

Jimmy's insides caught fire, how dare this man disrespect him in his house. The Cartone family played for keeps. He was hinting that his son move in and they would let him keep his daughter because she acted more black than Italian.

"Hey man, you must got a gun on you if you think I'm gonna let you take my son." Jimmy barked. "You don't run shit, this is my family and I will die for all three of them." Jimmy was pushing his luck in Mario's eyes. He wanted Jimmy dead. The only reason he was alive was because of Gina but he would go so far as to lie and give his father a reason to let him kill Jimmy.

"It's only fair Jimmy. He's black and Italian so they should both know our lifestyles but Giovanni on a more permanent basis. You should of stuck to your own kind Jimmy." Mario turned to walk off and then he turned back around. "Watch yourself, because it's gonna come a time when you realize that you're lucky to be alive. I got one piece of advice to give you. One slip up on your part and you're a dead man." Mario didn't give Jimmy a chance to respond as he walked out of the house.

Jimmy felt his world shake, he was just threatened by Gina's brother and if he would of mentioned it to her she would of made matters worse. Her family assured her that they had no quarrel with Jimmy as long as they saw the kids but Mario couldn't help it because he didn't make an agreement as far as he was concerned. Jimmy looked around the home he had with his wife and kids. He paced around the room thinking about what to do about the situation. The only thing he could do was talk to his brother about it in case things started to get out of hand.

Brian and Terell kept themselves occupied by throwing a football to each other in Tony's front yard. It had been a day since they witnessed their first dead body but neither child seemed too effected by it. They're young eyes were definitely introduced to a violent lifestyle due to what happened with

Marvin. Brian's face remained cold, there wasn't a trace of emotion in it. It was a bright sunny day and he couldn't even notice it. The heat was coming down on everybody, the summer feel made people come out of their shirts and into tank tops. Tony's neighborhood was quiet. It was higher middle-class but an isolated neighborhood. He owned a lot of land but a lot of it was just land.

"You can't tell anybody what happened to your dad Brian." Terell said while he threw the football to his best friend. He was as street smart as a ten year old kid could be and he felt he had to look out for Brian.

"I'm glad he's dead." Brian said coldly. "He won't be able to hit me now." Brian continued as he tossed the ball back to Terell. It was easy for him to speak of Marvin like that but he couldn't shake the image.

Brenda pulled her car up to the house and parked right behind Tony's Cadillac. She was a beautiful dark mocha complected woman. She had long legs and was slim but she was still curvy. She had short length hair that she kept straight with beautiful dark brown eyes. She dressed immaculately in a knee length dress with a halter top shirt because it was the end of August. She had on heels and when she walked you could hear the click clack down the block because of the anger in her steps.

She had come a long way from the woman that Marvin put down and abused. She went and got her degree and was working as an assistant to the D.A. but she was switching sides of the law to work with defense clients. She walked with pride and dignity and had a no-tolerance new attitude.

When she approached Brian she hugged him and told him to get in the car. Then she proceeded to march into Tony's house. She looked around the living room looking for Tony then she went into the bar area. Tony was sitting in his favorite chair behind the bar taking shots of brandy. It was obvious that he was extremely drunk. The look in his eyes was one of a madman but his exterior was calm and collected. The room still had a murderous stench to it through all the cleaning supplies that had been used in it. Brenda sighed and walked over to the bar, Tony looked up at her with a look of irritation because he knew what was coming.

"Before you say anything, you know why I killed him right?" Tony asked making sure she knew the story. "I gave him a fair warning, he didn't listen so I lost my cool."

Tony was feeling guilty about his rash decision, he wracked his brain trying to find a reason why he didn't just beat Marvin up, or shot him in the leg.

"So you did do it! What makes you think that I won't go to the police?" Brenda asked. Her and Tony both knew that she wouldn't of went to the police. In her heart she was glad Marvin was dead. The only reason she let Marvin see his son was because of Tony but at the same time she knew it wasn't Tony's choice to make if Marvin deserved to live or not.

"You're not God. On top of killing him you did it in front of my child and yours, if Monica was alive she would have killed you herself." Brenda barked.

Tony's eyes started to tear up, he was torn in his decision. He hated what he did to his friend but he still felt Brian was better off without him. He thought about the real reason he did it. He could have wanted to raise Brian himself, in his heart he felt that he would be a better father to Brian than Marvin.

"We make mistakes in life Brenda. You know Marvin wasn't shit and the beatings would have continued. I thought I could talk some sense into him but he wouldn't listen!" Tony exclaimed. She had an idea how bad the beatings were even though Marvin would have his son weeks at a time due to her old occupation as a stewardess. Tony would watch Brian more than Marvin because Marvin was always running the streets.

"I'm moving to Atlanta with my mother she's going to watch Brian while I get my practice started. If you want I'll send him back here every summer so you can see him. Weather you want to believe this or not, your son and mine will be affected for life by seeing you kill Marvin in cold blood, think about that." Brenda turned around and walked out of the house. Tony didn't say a word he just watched her leave and took another shot of brandy.

Brenda got to the bottom of the steps and seen Terell staring at her. She stopped and walked over to him and kneeled down to his eye level.

"When is Brian coming back?" Terell asked. Brenda's heart shook because she knew how close the two were but she remembered that Brian would be coming back in the summer which gave her comfort while she broke the poor kid's heart.

"Next summer, he's going to be back every summer to stay with you and your dad, okay." Terell just looked at her with a blank look on his face. He was hurt but was taught never to let your emotions show, just like Brian learned from his dad.

Brenda walked to her car and drove off. Brian and Terell stared at each other while they gave a slight head nod.

Tony had three establishments, two bars and one nightclub. One bar was called The Spot and it was found in the broken down part of the city. It had watered down drinks and all the street talk happened there. It was the location of the grapevine. People where went there were some of the biggest criminals in the city. The other two establishments were located in the same part of town where he lived. One was also called The Joint and it was a classier bar where regular successful blacks attended. Jimmy often went there with Gina. His nightclub was called The Palace and everybody in California came from entertainers to sports figures, even a small number of politicians would come and have drinks, food and good time.

It was night time and The Spot was dead, there were some regulars but no news that was circulating around the town. It wasn't important how many people were in there but the people who were in there were very important. Tony was sitting at his table in the right corner of The Spot with his two man crew Leroy and Eric. Tony had just decided to let Marvin rest in peace in his mind, he got to the point were the decision was made and the deed was done. His mind went back to it's comfort zone which was money and war tactics.

Eric was his right hand man, smart and cunning with a mean ruthless streak. He met Eric in jail about fifteen years ago and they've been running together every since Eric saved him from being killed by a skin head in the showers. To show Eric his gratitude Tony would share everything with him and fight along his side showing their solidarity. If a war was ever to happen Tony had the means to get a lot of soldiers on his team but Eric and Leroy were his two lieutenants.

Leroy was his muscle, he could fight with the best of them. He had been a boxer when he was twelve and was knocking out grown men by sixteen. He hooked up with Tony a couple of years ago after Tony spotted him beating up two men. One had a gun to his head. Leroy was the perfect muscle, he didn't ask questions and he followed directions to a tee which was something Tony liked very much in a lieutenant. There was something about his eyes that were unsettling. Tony saw it as pure rawness, but if you took a deep look it could definitely be interpreted as something else.

On the opposite side of the bar in a booth sat Vinnie Cartone who was Gina's youngest brother and Joey Delana who was the son of the Mob boss of California. The two of them were in a heated argument which stemmed from an attempt to make peace between the Delena family and the Cartones. The Cartone family were very lucrative and secretive in the drug business and only shared wealth with the other families. The way they handled business and stayed out of the eyes of the law were great. Because the Cartones were so hidden it brought more heat on the Delena family.

Carlo Delano's drug aspirations were suffering because of Cartone who was untouchable which angered Carlo Delena. The fact the Cartones could get away with not paying him because they earned so much for the other families angered Carlo Delena more than anything. After all, the Cartones were only connected and not made. After so many years a man can only listen to others for so long before he decides to take matters into his own hands. Vincent and Joey were there to come to an agreement and be the representatives speaking for the two families, but their conversation wasn't going the way they thought it would.

"It's only fair that the Delena family leaves the drug game alone. You guys got gambling, robbery, drugs and prostitution. How are we gonna earn out here if you put your hands in our pot!" Vincent exclaimed.

"We just want a percentage, were not trying to take over. You guys are getting a lot of money off that white powder." Joey responded.

Vincent knew what they were trying to do and so did the rest of his family. They were trying to put the Cartone's out of business.

"Look here bastard, if your pop thinks that you're gonna get the okay to take us out, you better think again because if you do there's gonna be a lot of angry families coming for you and you can bet that. Now get outta my face!" Vincent yelled. Joey held his rage in and felt that there was no point of continuing the conversation so he stood up still looking at Vincent

"Your family better learn how to reason or you won't be doing any thing." Joey pointed his finger in Vincent's face as he walked off.

Tony watched the whole thing and noticed that Vincent waived one of the waitresses into his direction. His mind went to instant strategy mode as he realized Vincent Cartone wasn't leaving and he and Joey Delena just had some words.

He was disgruntle about his situation and on top of being drunk he wanted to shake something up. He knew about the conflict that the two mob families were having and wanted them to focus on each other and not him. If that didn't work, there also could be a possibility that if he killed Vincent then Paul might take some time off, enough time for Tony to maneuver into a better connect.

"Eric, do you know who that is in the corner?" Tony asked. Eric started to whip his head around.

"Don't make it so obvious man." Tony warned.

"It's dark in here man, who is it?" Eric asked irritated about the guessing game that Tony was playing with him.

"That's Paul's youngest son. He was just getting into it with Joey Delena the Calli mob boss's son." Eric didn't do research on everybody getting money in his city. He didn't know about the brooding war between the two families over the drug game how they wanted to wipe each other out.

Tony watched Vincent closely as the waitress brought his drink back. Instead of slamming the drink down he noticed that Vincent was slowly drinking it as he puffed his cigarette deep in thought. Tony wondered why he was in this bar far away from his side of the tracks, but it didn't matter, this was the perfect opportunity to catch him slipping.

Eric and Leroy were so caught up in their conversation about some girl that they ignored the crazed look in Tony's eyes which they knew pretty well. Tony's wheels kept turning and he seen that the spot was getting emptier. He thought that now was the perfect time for him to make his move. He remembered that his car was the only one parked in the front of The Spot. Vincent was parked in the back which meant he was gonna leave out of the back door.

"Leroy I want you two to go to my trunk and get those sheets. Then go to the back, and stand on the side of the door. Eric, pop your trunk and start your car up." Tony ordered. Leroy and Eric looked confused. Tony noticed it so he further elaborated on his plan. "I gona shoot him when he walks out that door. Leroy, you wrap him up with the sheet and take him to Eric's trunk, do you get it?"

"How do you know that he's coming out of the back?" Eric asked. Tony gave him a look like he was appalled that Eric even questioned him.

"Don't worry about all that, let's get it man." Tony ordered.

Leroy and Eric got up and got the plan that Tony orchestrated in motion. Tony walked in the direction of Vincent and watched him like a hawk but in an indiscreet manner, he passed Vincent then walked out the back door and seen Leroy holding the sheet. Vincent finished off his drink and dropped a couple of dollars on the table as he walked in the same direction as Tony.

As soon as he stepped outside he didn't have a second to react before Tony shot him in the back of the head. In one fast swoop Leroy caught his lifeless body and wrapped him up in the sheet. Leroy threw the body on his shoulder while leaving a trail of blood all the way to Eric's trunk. Leroy made sure he covered Vincents blood drenched head as he put the body in the trunk. He slammed it shut and the three men sat in Eric's car and drove off.

As they were in the car Eric was the first to speak. "What was the point of that Tony?" Tony gazed at his friend like he was disappointed. He taught Eric a lot about warfare and his prodigy was letting him down when he asked questions like that. Tony only had one worry which was coming back and cleaning up the crime scene.

"It's called getting rid of the competition until they call a truce. Cartone may love money but he loves his family more. All we gotta do is watch out for the revenge factor, if we stay on our toes we'll be fine." Tony assured his comrades that he knew what he was doing. But deep in his mind he knew that seeds of a full blown out war would happen if Cartone found out is was him that killed his son instead of Joey Delena.

The Cartone mansion was huge. The layout was magnificent, paved with roses and different flower beds all over acres of land. It would take hours to landscape the property, all of Cartone's grandchildren loved to run around in it. He grew fruits and vegetables and had numerous cats around the house. There was one gravel paved road that circled around the main house. It came from a large gate that blocked his property off from the world. The inside of the house had many rooms, a study, kitchen, long hallways all lit up by fireplaces, along with a dinning room that was the size of a restaurant.

Paul, Mario and Tommy sat in the study which was their war room. It had a large desk with a chair behind it and two loveseats. There was no life or feeling in the room. The walls were blank, the only contents that weren't furniture were some papers, wine glasses, bottle of wine, and a wine bottle opener. It's purpose was to create an environment free of emotion so they all could think clearly.

Paul Cartone sat in his chair racking his brain for answers about the death of his son. When Vincent's body came up in the river and the funeral took place the whole family was at a stand still. Mario was enraged and on a warpath trying to find information. Tommy Cartone the second oldest child of Paul was pacing around the room trying to remain calm. Gina was at home with Jimmy and her kids she had been a wreck for weeks. Out of all her brothers Vincent was the one she was the closest to especially when she fell in love with Jimmy.

Tommy wasn't anywhere as large as his father or brother but he was stocky. He had a more American look to him compared to Italian. He his hair color was brown instead of black and he wore it curly not slicked back. He had strong features that stood out and the main one was his eyes. Tommy was convinced that it was the Delena family that killed Vincent because he heard of the meeting at the bar that Vincent was killed at. He was staring his father down with both of his hands pressed against his desk. His father who had been silent watched his son with serious eyes.

Paul wasn't quick to jump to any conclusion. He was a wise man who looked at every angle of any situation. His hurt ran deep but revenge filled his mind. For all he knew Vincent's murder could have been by some random junkie trying to rob him because of the fact he was in the black part of town.

"Pop it's obvious that Joey Delena killed Vinny, and I say we hit them back hard!" Tommy exclaimed.

Paul seen that his son was emotional but he knew that it was a strong possibility that the Delena family murdered Vincent and it was the most likely that it happened the way that Tommy was suggesting. He stood to his feet and walked around to the front of his desk. He poured himself a drink and looked over at Mario. He seen that his eldest son wasn't emotional as Tommy and was thinking more clear headed.

"What do you think Mario?" Paul asked. Mario knew some more information about another possible killer and now was the perfect time to reveal it.

"Pop, I got somebody coming by in a minute to give you some information about Vinny's murder." Mario stated. Then like clockwork Larry walked into the room.

Paul was in shock. He knew that out of all his kids that Mario was the most racist. Him and Tommy were against interracial couples, Gina and Vincent didn't see color but Mario hated black people period and now he had one coming into their home.

Larry had a plan to get in the dope game after Tony turned him down. He heard about the murder through the grapevine and seen this opportunity to get on. Larry knew the Cartone family would be grateful to him for handing them Tony which would allow him in the game and give him leverage against Tony. He also knew about Jimmy and Gina so that could give him some personal information to use.

"Mr. Cartone, I don't know if you know who Tony Taylor is, but he's a drug kingpin running the hood, in the coke game." Larry started. "He knows a lot about your family and he's the one that killed Vinny. Everybody is talking about it, he built some street credibility at the cost of your son's life." Larry knew he had Paul right were he wanted him.

Paul watched Larry closely. He had no idea about Tony and neither did his son's. That's where they slipped in war and Tony had the advantage. Larry knew that and all he was doing was waiting for their gratification and then switch the conversation to business. Paul and Mario were leaning towards believing Larry but Tommy wasn't buying it.

"Come on pop he just happens to come in here and say it was somebody else who killed Vinny, don't tell me your buying this garbage." Tommy said angrily. Larry kept looking at Paul when he spoke, because Paul's eyes never left him as Tommy was talking.

"If you don't believe me ask around yourself. No disrespect but you guys were kind of slipping not knowing about Tony he's been making a lot of money for years, and I know you like to keep your distance away from us, but if you knew about him you could of seen this coming." Larry said with a little nervousness, he knew that he could easily be killed by these gangsters if he spoke out of line, that's why he chose his words carefully.

Paul walked back behind his desk with his drink and sat back down. He put his fingers to his jaw line to his chin making a L with his index finger and his thumb. He was deep in thought for a second and then looked up at Mario.

"I believe him pop, I haven't heard of this cowboy but you have to admit somebody besides the Delena family might have the balls to kill Vinny, and look where he was at." Mario said.

"So by you coming forth with this information, you want something in return or are you just that generous." Paul asked suspiciously, he knew Larry had an agenda and he wanted to know what it was.

"I know we don't know each other but I'm trying to get in the game off credit." Larry said before Tommy interrupted him.

"You got a lot of balls nigger!" He exclaimed.

"If you give me some time I can have that whole part of the area locked for you and you won't need to step foot over there, but you know it's money in the hood, lots of it." Larry finished and he knew Paul and Mario was thinking hard about it.

"We can start you off with a key, you know who we are and now we know who you are. That's all I should have to say." Paul said while he pointed a finger at Larry. "Mario get him his stuff and Tommy you see if you can figure out how were going to handle this thing with this Tony character." Paul had his mind made up that he believed Larry, in the back of his mind he wanted to do whatever it took to avoid a war with the Delena family but still his instinct told him that Larry was telling the truth.

Tommy started to bring his argument back up but decided not to, he knew when his father's mind was made up. He didn't care if Joey Delena killed Vincent or not he wanted to see Carlo and his whole organization dead. Even if they hadn't killed Vincent he knew that they had some plans to come after the Cartone family and muscle them out of the drug game so they could have a monopoly on crime in California.

"Now if there isn't anything else I need to go pick up my grandson, Jimmy has agreed to let us keep Giovanni for some time." Paul spoke while he stood to his feet, and when Larry heard the name Giovanni he knew it couldn't be a coincidence that it could be another Jimmy with a son that had an Italian name, he also knew that Jimmy was married to an Italian woman.

"Excuse me Mr. Cartone, but are you talking about Jimmy Taylor the doctor." Larry couldn't wait to tell him that they were brothers.

"Yeah, that's my daughter's husband even though I can't say I'm happy about that." Paul responded wondering what Larry was getting at.

"Well, that's Tony's brother." Larry said with a slight smirk on his face. Mario felt his blood start to boil over. He walked up and got in Larry's face not to intimidate him but to make sure he heard Larry correctly. It seemed like the room was full of life at that moment. Those blank white walls turned red with Mario's rage, and blue with the stillness of Tommy and Paul who were shocked beyond belief.

"You mean to tell me that goody two shoes doctor has a brother who is a drug kingpin!" Mario spoke harshly while he stared Larry down.

"Yeah, it surprised the hell out of me, but it's true." Larry said.

"That's probably how that nigger got close to Vincent pop, Jimmy had to say something to him, I told you we should of killed him." Mario was normally known for being the calm one and Tommy was the emotional one but it seemed like the roles were reversed. Mario eyes started to tear up and he was pacing around the room.

Paul and Tommy were speechless, they felt betrayed, all the time they defended Jimmy because of the fact he wasn't caught up in their lifestyle and he was a respected man in the community almost made them disregard his color. If Jimmy would have been white he would have been perfect for their daughter and sister in the eyes of the Cartone family. But now with Larry revealing this information it made them believe that you couldn't trust any black person no matter what they did for a living, doctor or criminal.

Larry had just brought Jimmy into a situation that he had nothing to do with, he had no clue about Tony killing Vincent, and he was busy tending to his wife who was distraught over the death of her baby brother.

Jimmy sat on his couch watching television while he sipped his drink. He was listening to his Ray Charles record and looking at a game of chess that he started with himself on a dingy board with tattered pieces. It was his first chess set ever and he kept it around for that reason only, to play himself. His mind was racing, he could sense something big was going to happen. The music was soothing and the game relaxed him. He had caught the end of a Lakers basketball game before he decided to unwind and have a drink, which turned into a couple, which turned into a few, now he slowed down a bit. He was starting to question his decision to let Giovanni stay with the Cartone family for sometime because of the fact that Paul lost his son. But he felt that was the least that he could do. It bothered him how they favored Giovanni over Elana but he wanted to do whatever he could to smooth the hard time his wife and her family were gong through.

Out of all of Gina's brothers Vincent was the only one that was receptive to him. Vincent was kind of like Gina in a sense. He liked the African American culture which was one of the reasons why he hung out in the black bars and he also had a thing for black women. Him and Jimmy would share a few stories and have drinks on a few occasions. Vincent would tell Jimmy that he would get his family to come around one day.

Jimmy took a big gulp of brandy when the doorbell rang. He stood up and walked over to the door with a slow drag in his step. He look through the peep hole and seen his brother standing on the other side. He opened the door as Tony walked in with his head lowered. It had been a long time since Jimmy seen Tony look like a nervous wreck and it frightened him. He felt a shiver crawl up his spine because he knew that Tony had something terrible to tell him along with the fact that Tony rarely stepped foot in his house.

After an extended period of silence and stares Jimmy finally sparked up the conversation.

"What's wrong bro, what happened?" Jimmy just hoped Tony didn't say the one thing that could break his whole world, anything else would have been music to his ears. He hoped the reason Tony was looking so stressed was that he still felt bad about killing Marvin. Jimmy didn't agree with it but he didn't necessarily hate Tony for that, but he could tell that wasn't the case.

"I'm sorry bro, I didn't think about how it could affect you, I just saw an opportunity to come up and I took it." Tony started. "I killed the little Cartone." Tony said as he finally looked up at his older brother who had a scared look in his eyes. Jimmy instantly walked to the other side of his living room to his drink and drunk the rest that was in his glass. He slammed the cup down on the table and twirled back into his younger brother's direction.

"Dammit Tony, do you know how much pain you caused my wife man! You did it for a few extra dollars!" Jimmy exclaimed. He knew Tony was doing good for himself in the drug game so it boggled his mind why Tony felt like he needed to move in on the Cartone family who didn't want anything to do with Tony's terrirrtory.

"Cartone's time is over!" He yelled. If you didn't get mixed up with them I could have been took all of them out, but you had to marry his daughter." Tony said trying to defend himself against his brother's wrath. "I'm just letting you know what's up and if any of 'em try something I'll kill they whole family! I'm sorry to get you involved in this Jimmy but they don't know we're brothers, and they don't even know who I am as long as we keep it that way you won't have nothing to worry about. But as long as you stay married to that woman your are gonna have to worry." Tony said as he walked over to the table with the brandy on it and poured himself a nice amount of Brandy and quickly drunk it.

"You don't see how your ways hurt other people besides yourself man. I never judged you for what you do because you're my brother and I love you. But when you put my family in jeopardy then that's where I draw the line, you either leave this alone or I'm walking away from you, bottom line."

The calm mellow mode that was once in the air had gone and neither man could notice how the Ray Charles record was skipping in the background.

The words hurt Jimmy's soul just coming out of his mouth. He loved his brother with all of his heart but there had to come a time where enough was enough. He seen the hurt in Tony's face but he also seen the pride in his eyes, he knew Tony loved him but this vendetta against his wife's family was fueling Tony. It made him feel alive to be going after the top guys in his line of work and he wanted Cartone's spot no matter who he had to step on to get it and that's the way it was going to be.

"Look Jimmy, I'm wrong for not thinking about how this situation would affect you, but that's all I was wrong for I wasn't wrong for what I did, I killed Vincent but . . . ." As Tony said the last four words of that sentence Gina, Elana and Giovanni came into the door just to hear them. Gina looked up at Tony speechless and within three seconds she lunged at Tony slapping him in his face. Un-phased by the blows Tony allowed her to do it. Jimmy grabbed his wife as she cried hysterically, Tony looked at her for a second before walking out of the house. Jimmy hugged his wife, but she only let him for a few seconds before pushing him off of her.

"Kids go to your room." Jimmy ordered as he poured himself another drink.

"What are you going to do about this Jimmy?" Gina asked with her hands on her hips. "Your brother killed my brother so what are you going to do?" Gina was staring a hole through her husband. Jimmy couldn't say anything he just kept drinking, this whole situation was eating at him.

"What do you expect me to do, call the police and send my brother to jail. Once your family finds out about this, which they will, they'll probably come looking for him." Jimmy knew his words weren't helping but he didn't know what to say anyway so it didn't matter to him.

"You got that right, it will be one less nigger walking around when I tell my papa." Gina said, but the word came out so fast she couldn't stop it. She instantly turned and seen the look Jimmy was giving her and tried to keep her wall up although she felt bad.

"Look, I know your upset but don't you ever degrade me or somebody I love with that word Gina, I love you, but I won't tolerate that. If that's how you feel I will leave and your family would have done what they set out to do which is getting' rid of me." Jimmy walked to the hall closet and grabbed his coat, as he put it on Gina kept pretending like she wasn't affected by Jimmy leaving. It wasn't until he got to the door when she dropped the act.

"Jimmy wait! I'm sorry but you got to understand where I'm coming form. My brother is dead and it's Tony's fault, I know what kind of business that all of them are in but you can't expect me to be okay with this." Gina said.

"I don't, and I know this is hard for you, but we have to take our family and get out of this, because if this is the route they want to go, let's let them deal with it and just leave, after." Jimmy forgot about the promise he made to Paul.

"After what?" Gina asked.

"I forgot that I promised Paul that Giovanni could stay with him for a week or two." Jimmy wanted to go back on his word but felt that it would be wrong. Gina automatically knew it was a bad idea. Once they got him around they would keep using Vincent's death as a way to get Jimmy to allow them to keep Giovanni which is what they wanted in the first place and Gina didn't want that to happen.

"No Jimmy, they're trying to use Vinny to make you feel sorry for them and keep our son, don't let them take him at all." Gina said.

"No honey, I'm not giving him away, our son probably will help him deal with the loss of his son that's all, and when a couple of weeks is up we can go, I'm sure I can get a transfer and we can go to New York or a place far away from here." Jimmy said re-assuring his wife that he hadn't given his son to her father, but Gina wasn't convinced and she was tired of arguing so she went into they're bedroom to get some rest, leaving Jimmy to sit in his chair and left him to slamming down shots of brandy like he had been doing all day.

Another ten minutes passed and another knock on the door startled Jimmy who was extremely drunk at this point. He staggered to his feet and groaned while he made his way over to the door and looked through the peep hole and seen Mario standing on the other side. He opened the door and met an angry look on Mario's face. Inside he was laughing at the pudgy man, but on the outside he showed a look of concern as he stared back at him.

"Drowning your sorrows huh Jimmy?" Mario asked as he invited himself in looking around the home. "Is my sister and the kids here?" He was hoping that Jimmy said no, but was disappointed when he received the answer because he had intentions on blowing Jimmy's brains out luckily he had his silencer with him. He paced around the living room for a second then looked at Jimmy.

"Gina is sleep in the back, so what can I do for you?" Jimmy asked even though he got a nervous feeling that the alcohol couldn't even cover up.

"I'm here to ask about your brother Tony." Mario watched for Jimmy's response but didn't really see one. "I hear he's the one that wacked Vinny." Jimmy walked over to his bottle and poured another shot.

"My brother's business is his, I stay out of it. If that's what happened I didn't know about it." Jimmy tried to keep his composure but he knew how bad Mario wanted to kill him and he got the feeling that today was the day. He thought about going back with the kids thinking that Mario wouldn't be crazy enough to kill him in front of his niece and nephew but something inside of him felt that he shouldn't. He couldn't read the man to save his life, there was a calm crazed look about him.

Mario was still set in his decision but he wanted to see Jimmy squirm because he seen the fear in him for the first time and was enjoying it. It also made him believe the Jimmy had some guilt and that Tony was the one to kill Vincent. The fact that Jimmy was so plastered took away from the enjoyment but that wasn't going to ruin this moment that he'd been waiting for years to approach.

"I'll be right back." Mario said coldly as he walked into the bathroom. He looked in the mirror and a grin went across his face as he pulled out his gun and a silencer, he put the silencer on and flushed the toilet to insinuate that he used the bathroom, he then ran the water to further play out his trick.

Jimmy sat down with his bottle and his eyes closed, the alcohol had his nerves calm and he started praying to himself, when Mario came out he stood up and his eyes got wide as he saw the gun pointed at him.

"Don't worry Jimmy this ain't for you." Mario said calmly, he didn't want Jimmy to be alarmed.

Those words made Jimmy relax a bit, but he was far from relieved. He still wondered why he had a gun pointed at him and assumed Mario was playing head games. He then thought if he was going to die he would have been dead which is something he had learned about wise guys from being married to the daughter of a full fledge gangster. He wanted to call for Gina but he was slowly accepting his fate.

Mario and Jimmy watched each other for a second before Mario spoke. "I want you to come with me Jimmy and pay my brother a visit at his gravesite." Mario spoke in a monotone.

He knew then his life was over and he couldn't make a run for it. He thought one last time to scream for Gina but for some reason he was content with dying. "Sure thing Mario just let me grab my jacket." Jimmy responded. As he walked past Mario and to the hall closet, Mario closed his eyes and shot Jimmy in the back five times. Jimmy moaned almost silently as his body landed in the closet without a thud. Mario walked over and put one more bullet in the back of his head, then looked down the hall to see if anybody had came out. When he saw that the coast was clear he walked up and spat on Jimmy before walking out of the house.

After a few minutes Giovanni came out of his room and walked down the hall. "Dad!" He called out. When he didn't get an answer he noticed that the hall closet door was ajar so he walked over and saw his father laying there lifeless with bullet holes in his back

"Mom!" The boy cried out several times before Gina woke up. She came out the of the room cursing her son out until she stopped in front of the door and seen her husband slain.

She started crying hysterically and trying to lift Jimmy up. She finally got him out of the closet, as she hugged and rocked him in her arms between sobs. Elana heard the commotion and came out of the room. Once she saw what her brother and mother saw she joined in with the moaning and crying. The three of them sat around their dead loved one as a family.

Tony sat in his bar watching the news with a bottle of brandy in front of him. He had been stunned for a week after hearing about his brother's murder and now he was ready for revenge. It was the same day that he was over there which made him hurt more because the last time he saw his brother alive they were in a argument. He knew who was responsible for it and felt like Jimmy was just an innocent by-stander. To him Cartone was playing dirty because Tony killed somebody who was in the life and that's part of the game but Jimmy had nothing to do with their lifestyle. He had been crying for days, and drinking more than ever before.

He couldn't leave his bar area, different women would come over to his house and cook for him, along with straightening his place up. His home was very grim but he didn't mind the feeling because it matched his heart and mind.

"The community is still in shock from the death of Dr. James Taylor." The news reporter started. "He had saved countless lives and was the most prominent doctor in the state. He will surely be missed, his killer hasn't been apprehended and police are still looking." Tony turned the television off and threw his empty glass at the wall shattering it. He looked up in the doorway that led to his main house and saw a curvaceous woman standing there, as he looked closer he recognized her as Gina Cartone.

"What are you doing here?" He asked with optimism.

"I need to talk to you." She responded as she walked into the bar. "Can I sit down?" She knew it was a possibility that he would tell her to leave but she wanted to take her chances. Tony pointed to a seat as he pulled a cigarette out and lit it. It was only out of curiosity that he didn't tell her to take a hike and never step foot in his house again.

"Are you gonna offer me a drink?" Gina asked. Tony made a gesture with his hand as to say help yourself. Gina grabbed the bottle and glass that set next to it and poured a drink, she downed the shot with precision before she spoke. "I want you to kill him." She said with a twinge of coldness in her voice. Tony was in shock but played it off.

"Who?" He asked, he knew it was one of her brothers she was talking about but he wanted to know which one, or maybe it was her father she was talking about.

"Mario, it was Mario who killed Jimmy. I know you killed Vinny because of this dirty business, and I know Jimmy had nothing to do with it. So kill Mario and leave the rest of my family alone, can you do that?" Gina was crying at this point she never would have imagined that she'd be setting up her own brother's death but every since Jimmy died she couldn't sleep or eat and she wouldn't get any rest until Mario paid for what he did.

Tony would love nothing more to kill the man who took his brother for him but he had to think about the set-up aspect of this all. She could be trying to catch him off guard and make him feel comfortable so he could be food on the plate of her family, or was she really that heart broken over Jimmy that she would actually go so far to have her own brother killed?

"You don't mean this shit, go home Gina, Jimmy and Vinny are both gone let's just let this situation play out the way it is." Tony was still trying to read this woman that's why he kept his little masquerade going.

"No!" Gina yelled. You don't have to look into two pairs of eyes and see Jimmy everyday. I feel like he's talking to me through his children telling me to avenge his death. I can't believe he actually turned his back to my brother. That coward shot my husband in the back! If your not going to help me then your just as much as a coward as they are, if your not going to avenge your brother's death then I'll do it for you." Gina stood up and turned to walk out before Tony put a tight grip on her arm.

He heard enough, the emotion and the look in her eyes spoke to him deeply. He could feel her energy and hurt as it was part of him and he knew she was actually serious. Gina's heart rate started to slow down a little and her breathing got more calmer by the second.

"Sit down." Tony told her, she sat down and stared at Tony waiting to see what he was going to say next. Tony ashed his cigarette and looked up at her.

"Okay I'll do it, do you got some kind of information that I should know, like where he hangs out at, where would he be the most comfortable." Tony asked. He hoped she could make this as easy on him as possible. He watched as Gina went through her purse she pulled out half of a piece of paper.

"He's going to be on his honeymoon this weekend in San Francisco, this is the hotel address and room number where he's going to be staying. The rest you have to figure out." Gina said handing Tony the paper.

It was perfect for Tony, she basically did all the leg work, the rest of the hit was going to be child's play for a man who was as strategic as he was.

"That's going to be easy, now look I'm going to do this by myself okay." Tony said. Gina shook her head, there was no way she wasn't going to be there.

"I'm going too Tony. I may not be in there when you do it, but I'm going to be waiting in the car. I'm giving you all this information at least I can be there!" Gina exclaimed. Tony seen it as pointless to argue so he left it alone. He refilled his glass and raised it up. "This is for my brother." He said. Gina looked at him for a second poured a glass and raised it. "And my husband." They did a toast solidifying their temporary alliance and then took a drink.

Tony and Gina sat in the driver and passenger seat in a rented car in San Francisco at the hotel where Gina's brother Mario was staying with his wife. Gina was chewing a piece of gum while her whole body was in a state of the jitters. Tony was finishing off a cigarette as he pulled out a little baggie filled with cocaine. The only time Tony did cocaine was when he was going to do a planned out murder. This was different than Vincent's murder because that was more of a desperate, drunk attempt to make a statement. This on the other hand was more than business, it was personal and the coke helped calm him down.

Tony looked over at Gina's focused face but could see her nervousness. Her thighs and legs were shaking so he reached over and touched her thigh. She immediately stopped and looked up at Tony with a surprised look on her face until she realized it wasn't a sexual pass, it was an attempt to get her to calm down.

"Could you not do that, we need you clear headed?" Gina asked as she watched Tony indulge himself into some coke.

Tony ignored her as his mind went into focus mode. He watched the hotel and checked his watch as he waited for the time to commit the murder. Gina looked around the lot wondering when Tony was going to make his move.

"Don't worry, if I don't do this shit my mind will be all over the place. This actually keeps me level headed. I'm not gonna mess this up, trust me." Tony declared as he reached over her lap and opened the glove compartment. He pulled out his gun and slid the silencer on it then closed the compartment. Then he tossed his cigarette butt and slid on his gloves. He opened the door, stepped out of the vehicle and put the gun in his back pocket. Gina watched anxiously waiting for the moment to see him coming back down telling her the job had been completed and her husband's death had been avenged.

Tony walked through the parking lot and his heart was beating steadily unlike his two most recent killings Vincent and Marvin. Tony didn't enjoy murder but something about it made him feel powerful. There were two types of murders in his eyes some you regret and some you don't, this was one of those times he wouldn't even give murder a second thought. He thought about the look in Mario's eyes when he realized he was going to have his last breath. He wondered what he would think, if he would be kicking himself for a split second for killing his brother.

Tony walked into the front door of the hotel and past the clerk who was talking on the phone. He walked to the elevators and pressed the up button. As the elevator doors reached the first level and opened up for him, he slid in and pressed the seventh floor. His heart beat started to pick up as the doors closed and the pull from the rise in height of the elevator started. It stopped at the third floor and a young Latino girl walked inside and pushed the fifth floor then looked up at him. Tony looked back down and smiled at the young girl relieved that she wasn't going to the same floor as he was.

She had two pigtails and you could see the amazement of Tony in her eyes. It was the feeling like she was looking at her father who could have been like him. A gangster but a loving man who lived his life right according to his family love. Tony thought about the magnetic attraction she had for him in the short time they spent in the elevator.

The elevator came to a stop at the fifth floor and the girl walked off giving Tony one more look and a smile. He watched the doors close again and started thinking about the kill. It was seconds away and he knew that Mario wouldn't be expecting this. He would be with his wife in anniversary bliss then BAM!

His mind was laughing like it was some kind of satanic voice in his head. He heard the final ding as he reached his destination and walked out of the elevator.

He looked to his left and right in search for the room 704, his heart started beating faster now, it was pumping, the urge of the kill had his heart busting out of his chest and when he reached the door his heart skipped a beat. He just stared at the room for a moment. He heard faint voices on the other side of the door. He could barely tell that is was a male and a female. He heard a little bit of laughter.

He knocked on the door and anticipated for it to open. After a couple of seconds he heard foot steps approaching the door, then the slurring words of a woman became more evident which was perfect. Drunk people usually aren't as alert to danger as sober ones which made his task more easy.

"Who is it?" a woman's voice called out.

"Management mam, we got a complaint." Tony said in his best business tone.

"A complaint about what, we aren't even being loud!" She exclaimed.

"Can you just open up and let me tell you what it is about, it'll only take a second." Tony responded. The woman who was Mario's wife opened the door to a fist knocking her backwards, and then a quick shot to her head followed it, he closed the door as he entered the room. Mario tried his best to get to his gun but wasn't quick enough because Tony had already made his way into the large sized room and had his gun pointed right at Mario.

"Too slow fat man." Tony walked slowly in the room as Mario backed away from his gun and sat up. He folded his arms and tried to intimidate Tony showing no fear which was his only option. Images of Jimmy's dead body and the funeral were running through his mind this would be the sweetest killing ever.

"Vincent was business but you killing my brother was personal. Jimmy wasn't involved in our game you went against the rules white boy. You know what, the made mobsters go everywhere together, even anniversaries. Guess that's why the Delena family hate you guys, you think you're too good for the mob." Tony said coldly, he was keeping his cool so nobody would notice the confrontation. If he started yelling the management would be called for real. "What do you have to say for yourself?" Tony asked even though it didn't matter.

"What does your black ass know about us." Mario said almost laughing

"I know you don't have anyone hear to save you." He responded.

"Just kill me, I got enough satisfaction killing your brother, I just got a question for you nigger, how did you find me?" Mario watched Tony, he knew he was dead but he didn't think anybody was good enough to follow him that well.

A big smile spread across Tony's face, he was glad to answer that question for Mario. "Your sister. Turns out she's more loyal to my brother than you which should tell you something. She told me it was your anniversary, where you were going to be, she basically handed you to me on a silver platter. Then you sitting here getting drunk made it that much easier, I guess it's safe to say you were slippin' fat man. Now revenge is so lovely when you're the one holding the gun." Tony kept walking closer to Mario.

"Just hurry up and do it, you should of seen the look on Jimmy's face when I wacked him. It was priceless, don't worry my father and brother are gonna make sure your black ass . . . ." Tony shot Mario five times in his chest the same amount of times he shot Jimmy in the back. He left blood all over the sheets, the silencer covered up the noise so nobody heard a thing. Tony quickly turned around and walked out of the room closing the door behind him.

He swiftly walked to the elevator doors pushing the down button repeatedly until the doors finally opened then he stepped in the elevator. He felt alive and happy vengeance was his. That moment was more pleasurable than sex or counting millions of dollars, it was the ultimate satisfaction and he got it.

As the elevator went to the bottom floor he stepped out unnoticed by everybody, the people in the lobby went about their business not knowing there were two murdered people upstairs and the man who killed them was walking out of the doors about to get away with the crime.

Tony jogged through the parking lot and back to the rental car as he opened the door he met Gina's wide eyes with a smile on his face. The smile was all she needed to see to know that her brother was no longer alive. She turned her head straight forward with a blank look on her face. Once Tony started the car and drove off she remained silent the whole ride.

⸻

Tony was at The Spot with Eric and Leroy. Leroy was gambling at pool like he usually does, and Eric was telling Tony a story about some female he was with last night. Tony was half way listening to his second in command's story, smiling at certain funny parts Eric would say but his mind was on alert mode because he was worried about the aftermath of what him and Gina did in San Francisco.

Paul and Tommy found out everything they needed to know about Tony and they knew about his businesses. They also watched The Joint and the Palace and found out that he frequently visited The Spot more than any other one which made it easy for him to get to. Tony felt the most comfortable there, he wanted to be around what he considered "real people."

The Spot was packed on a Saturday and females were eying the fellows all night. Getting women was no problem when you had money and power especially in a place like that which was filled with two dollar hustlers, and penny pushers, but those pennies did add up to dollars. There was a fine young chocolate woman catching Tony's attention in the corner of The Spot but she was there with one of the few Italian dudes in the bar. He kept looking at Tony as if he recognized him but it wasn't obvious enough for Tony to react to or even think about for that matter. If Tony's mind wasn't occupied or if he wasn't drunk he would have already been on him.

"Are you listening to me?" Eric asked once he realized Tony wasn't even paying attention.

"Yeah I heard you, she was sexier than Pam Grier, I don't believe it but that's what you said." Tony responded starting to notice the Italian man more and more. "But do you see that wop over there mugging us man? Do you think he with the Cartones?" Tony was getting paranoid and Eric could see.

"Nah man, you just trippin' over what happened with Cartone's son man don't worry about it." Eric re-assured him. But Tony wasn't satisfied with that answer.

"That's how you get killed man, I'm bout to get to the bottom of this." Tony stood up and walked towards the back of the bar where the couple were standing. He pulled his gun out and without warning he started pistol whipping the man down to his back. Blood and teeth went flying and two of his friends tried to rush Tony but before they could touch him Eric and Leroy were right there grabbing them and making it a full blown brawl. Tony only stopped to catch his breath then resumed with the beating he was giving out.

"Did Cartone send you?" He asked in a yell over and over between blows to the head. This time he only stopped to let the man respond. After three seconds of the man just breathing harshly he would resume kicking him in his ribs and chest.

Nobody in The Spot tried to jump in or call the cops in fact some people were egging the fight on, when white people got beat up in black neighborhoods sometimes the feeling of sympathy was non-existent. Tony stopped attacking the man but Leroy and Eric continued to beat their opponents so Tony felt like getting more aggression out started helping Eric because he figured that Leroy didn't need it. Eric was holding his own but Leroy was the muscle his instinct told him to join in with Eric.

Moments later machine gun shots filled through The Spot and people were getting shot left and right. Tony dropped to the ground crawled over to the side of a jukebox and used it for cover. It was like they weren't running out of ammo and Tony looked up with his gun out and spotted Leroy behind the bar. He desperately looked for Eric and when he found him he started to tear up because the grotesque sight of his best friend was bad enough to make his stomach turn.

The shots stopped and Tommy along with three other guys started to come in The Spot. Leroy and Tony were thinking the same thing because before Tommy could even make his way through the door they were on the way to the back door.

As they were outside running to Tony's car they heard more shots and it seemed like the bullets were getting closer and closer to them. Tony got to the driver side of his car just as Leroy arrived at the passenger side.

"Hurry up man!" Leroy screamed as the shots came in striking range.

"I'm trying!" Tony yelled back.

He finally got the key into the car door and got it I open, he reached over and unlocked it and as Leroy got in. A bullet hit the open door. Leroy closed the door as Tony started the car and put his foot to the petal. Shots busted his window and shattered his glass and hit the back and the bottom of his car but the two man escaped with all their limbs but the war wasn't over yet, not by a long shot.

The Year was 1983 and Brian approached the bus station in Los Angeles California. Just liked his mother promised Tony and Terell, Brian came back and spent the summer with them for the next eight years. Not only was he excited to see them but he would always pick up his summer fling with Elana. The two of them got close over the years and he wanted to surprise her with the news that he was coming back for good to finish out his senior year in high school.

Brian was the same kid as he was when he left. He was extremely intelligent and that's where his confidence lay. He was still somewhat misguided like your average eighteen year old but he had an amazing grasp on life. He was handsome but stood short in size. He had a slim build and a slim face with short cut hair. His eyes were large and inviting, and his nose wasn't too wide or skinny. Females weren't taken back by his appearance because he was more of the adorable type then the sexy type of male from a woman's perspective.

A lot had changed since the death of Mario. Tommy and Paul had a full blown out war with Tony, neither side being able to take the others life but money and power went up and down between the two. The chess game eventually came to a stalemate until Terell took over the family business. Tony in a way lost the heart for it when Eric and Jimmy died, but maintained the business because that was all he knew how to do.

Since Larry had made the deal with the Cartone's he moved in on some of Tony's territory so a small feud between them was brewed but Larry turned out to be a slick man at war games himself so Tony also dipped his hands in other hustles besides the drug game. Tony had to give Larry credit though, he cleaned himself up and became a worthy adversary to his surprise. If only he gave him a shot that day in his bar then he wouldn't be an opponent but a friend.

As far as the kids, well that was a different story. Terell became a menace to society. He had braids and a slim face like his father's. He was a handsome kid but he had the most ruthless eyes and a scar on his face similar to Tony Montana's from being smashed in the face with a bottle by some grown man when he snuck in The Spot at twelve years old. He was a livewire who had a temper worse than his father's. Terell's only soft spot was for Brian. He always felt like he needed to take care of Brian. He admired him for his courage and intelligence, and he would put anybody underneath the ground if they laid a hand on him. Their bond had grown deep, from best friends to real brothers and he was ecstatic that his brother was home for good.

Brian had seen a lot of things in Atlanta but it was a different lifestyle that he was accustomed to in California. Every summer he loved coming back to see Terell, Tony and Elana. He was ready to graduate with a perfect G.P.A. He never knew what it felt like to fail at anything he put his mind to and books was probably the most simple thing to him. He was also street smart and learned that from Tony and Terell. He referred to Tony as his father which irritated his mother knowing the history and still holding a grudge with Tony for murdering Marvin. But she allowed it because no matter what she said Brian loved Tony as his father and in her heart she knew that the love was the same. Brian was happy to be at home full time and getting the information about the fast life in L.A.

Elana and Giovanni lives went in total opposite directions. Elana turned into a very beautiful young lady with a fondness for music and dancing. She was a head turner with the grace of an angel. When a lot of girls said they were waiting and remaining a virgin she really was. Many men tried to get next to the eighteen year old from all ages but she maintained he virtuosity. She had eyes for one man which was Brian and even though many summers Brian tried to get in between the sheets with her she still didn't even though she had deep feelings for him.

The difference between him and others was that it wasn't about the sex and he could control himself, he kept it respectful. When he was in Atlanta he had girls but when he was in L.A. he only had eyes for his prize and that is what Elana was. She was a trophy for any man and no matter what she said about hating that title she loved it She identified more with her African American side. She didn't see the Italian part of her family often because she still remembers the tension between her father and them but she didn't know the whole story. Tony promised Gina they wouldn't discuss the family history with the kids they would just leave it at that.

Giovanni on the other hand was somewhat of a tortured soul, who was a drifter. Besides his cousin Henry who was Tommy's son and their crew he was by himself. Him and Terell were cousins but they never spoke to each other as far as they were concerned they were enemies. They knew the family history and they knew that there were alliances made and family or not there was hatred. Elana and Terell were very close. Terell had to kill a couple of older dudes who tried to rape Elana one time and while her own brother accused her of dressing like a whore, Terell came and made sure they wouldn't attempt to rape nobody ever. It's like what Mario said about the twins years ago was actually the truth Giovanni identified more with his Italian side and Elana identified more with her black side.

"What's up man?" Terell called as Brian got in the car. He drove off and turned the corner headed to his father's house. "So no more every summer visits, you're finally back for good right?" Terell asked even though he already knew the answer.

"Yeah. I'm ready to get school done with, to tell you the truth it's starting to bore me." Brian said in a conceited tone.

"That's because you can do it with your eyes closed. You just as good at books as I am in the streets." Terell always reminded Brian about how smart he was so little comments like that was expected to come from his mouth as far as Brian was concerned. He felt Terell did it to keep Brian focused on what he needed to do with his life which was get a degree and make something out of himself.

"You're pretty good at what you do but you don't get bored." Brian said trying to start a debate with his brother, Terell sensed it and nipped it in the bud.

"Hey man, I see what you doing. We've had this conversation and the deal was I'll tell you all about what's going on in these streets but under no circumstances do you try and get cute and drop out of school." Terell was pointing his left index finger at Brian as he drove, there was a little irritation in his tone but it was more concern then anything else.

"Calm down man, I know. I'm talking about high school. It's boring, I can't wait for college, you know what I'm sayin'. It's only a year left but it's been easy for the past three years and it's fuckin' over. But anyway what's been going on around here lately." Brian asked trying to change the subject. It was always some kind of dirt going on and he wanted the information.

"Pops let me get full control of the business now so I got my own crew. Mac and Timothy, a two-man crew just like he had back in the day. We in the game deep, we pretty much got his clientele but we in competition with Larry. Mac is a savage with a rep for killing. Timothy is soft but he's smart and I use him for anything that got something to do with brains, like numbers. I could of used you for that but you got too much going for yourself. I never introduced you to them because it's now getting to that organized status." Terell said.

"Do you trust them?" Brian asked, he had a big issue with trust he only trusted a handful of people and his own father wasn't one of them. He used to always worry about Terell or Tony getting killed by somebody close to them, so while Terell was talking about people in his circle Brian automatically starting building a watchful eye in his mind about these guys.

"Then, just last week somebody popped Paul Cartone in the head and had blood dripping in his spaghetti." Terell said with a slight smirk. "They've been questioning pop about it all week, they even got at me a couple of times, but them punk ass pigs ain't said nothin to the Delena family yet. Terell was playing detective at this point, he had his father's war time sense. He knew things was about to get sticky and it wasn't the right time for Brian to come back but what doesn't kill you makes you stronger.

"What about Giovanni, what's up with him. Has he had the black slapped back into him yet?" Brian asked. There was something about the way Giovanni did an about face after Jimmy died that bothered him. Giovanni wasn't a pro-black activist but he still had a little bit of flavor to him. Every summer that Brian returned back to L.A. it seemed like slowly but surely it was fading. Brian wasn't necessarily a racist but it was kind of odd, like Giovanni's mind was being pulled in a certain direction and he wasn't making decisions about his life on his own.

Giovanni did think with his own mind though and to him he saw blacks killing each other and it seemed like Italians had more of a family tradition. Even though Tony and his father were close they were only two individuals out of a city filled of black people who were killing and stealing from their own family members which was family love he didn't want.

"That's my cousin but we don't speak at all, he made his choice on the color line." Terell said, you could tell it bothered him that he wasn't close with his first cousin the only male one he had. That's why Brian's relationship was so important to him. "I ain't going to lie though, I heard he was nice with the fist. A couple of cats I knew from back in the day came back from Juve` sounding like little girls talking about how some mixed cat was busting all three of them up, turned out to be him." Terell had a splash of pride in his voice speaking about Giovanni but that's how far as it went, it didn't change anything.

"What about my lady, how she doing?" Brian said referring to Elana. He was itching to ask about her but didn't want to seem to desperate because he knew how Terell was. If he was too anxiousness to see her or even hear about her well-being, Brian would be called all kinds of suckas.

"I don't know what you did or how you got my cousin stuck on you. For the last couple of weeks you're all she talks about." Terell said in amazement.

"I already told you, I'm the total package, the complete man, that get's them every time. I'm gonna marry her bro." Brian said staring down Terell.

"Whateva man." Terell said chuckling he couldn't wrap his mind around the concept of marriage or even being with one woman. He turned the corner to where his father's house was and pulled into the driveway. Brian got out of the car and reached into the backseat to grab his bags. He threw one bag over his shoulder and picked the other one up as he walked towards the house.

"Thanks for the help man." Brian said to Terell sarcastically.

"Look, I'm gonna help you out with the door." Terell said laughing. He held the door open for Brian as he walked passed and set the bags down by the door. He heard Rick James playing in the bar area and removed his shades. The two of them walked to the bar area and seen Tony sitting in his same spot with his bottle of brandy in front of him, smoking a cigarette.

The front room of Tony's house still was the same but the bar was a completely different area. It had a more party vibe to it. The music was loud and the sliding door was open. Tony seemed like he had more life to him even after last year when Brian visited, the feeling was different.

Tony and Leroy were having drinks in the bar talking about the Scarface movie that just had came out. It had every gangster in America talking.

"I've seen that movie ten times man, it's a good flick." Leroy said while he downed his shot. "I tell you what, that's how you come up until he got that big head and tried to take on Sosa." Tony shook his head, he liked the movie but his black activism poked it's head out.

"They should of made Tony black man, why it gotta be a Cuban killing the game like that. A black man would have did it right, and there's more blacks making major dough off coke than anybody anyway." Tony always argued that black people are the best at everything.

"Your average man would of did the same thing, got rich, got to big headed and got killed." Leroy argued.

"Whateva man, you the same man that said Jake Lamatta was a better fighter than Sugar Ray Robison why should I have any kind of debate with you." Tony responded waiving Leroy's comment off.

"He was tougher which made him better." Leroy stated as he poured another shot and slammed it as soon as Terell came waltzing through the door.

"Look who I got with me pop." Terell announced. Tony looked and seen Brian, he instantly got a smile on his face. Brian walked over to him and gave him a hug while he was still sitting down. Brian pulled up a chair next to him. Tony poured Brian a shot and slid it in front of him.

"Have a shot with your old man." Tony said while he put his hand on Brian's shoulder. Brian obliged and cringed his face up after the harsh liquor hit his throat and slid down it. "So where you going to school next year, college man." Tony questioned hoping he would say somewhere in California.

"USC, they got a good journalism program, I'm gonna write articles about this corrupt system we got here in this crooked country." Brian said.

"You hear that Terell, that's what I've been talking about all these years man, my son the activist!" Tony was excited, he imagined Brian being like Malcolm X, he was proud. Terell had no interest in social issues, all he respected was money. He didn't care if it was white money or black money all he saw was green.

"Sorry to bust your bubble Brian but there ain't no way one man is going to make a difference." He said in a cynical tone.

"That's why you need millions of black people to stand up and do something to make a difference but you'll see when we get this movement going." Brian said, he heard it all before from people like Terell so he found a way not to argue his point but show his point by making a change.

"You can do whatever you want son so don't let nobody get you off track." Tony said as he poured a shot for himself and his two sons. Terell walked over to the bar after he seen the third glass and the three of them raised them up.

"To money and power." Terell said as they slammed the shot glasses down.

"Don't forget happiness." An angelic voice called from the bar area entrance. Brian looked over and saw an image of perfection. Elana Cartone Taylor, the love of his life was standing at the doorway with her hand on her hip and a smile on her face. She stood there and watched them for a second before she walked into the bar area to give hugs out.

When she made her way to Brian the two took a moment staring at each other. "So I hear you're in town for good now, and going to my school." Brian nodded his head. "Do you still get straight A's every year." Brian nodded his head for a second time. "Stop trying to be cute. Are you going to the carnival tonight?." She asked.

"I didn't know about a carnival." Brian responded looking at Terell.

"I didn't want to tell you because I know if you knew she'll be there you might want to go and I don't want to go." Terell said as he poured another shot, he was developing a drinking habit like his old man but it didn't bother him because when it came down to handle business he didn't drink one drop of liquor unlike a lot of gangsters who always got liquored up before they did some dirt.

"Now I know and if you ain't going I am." Brian said. Terell started to argue but even though he looked out for Brian he also knew that when he wanted to do something there was no changing his mind so he left it alone. He broke some weed down on the bar table and grabbed a joint paper.

"Suit yourself." Terell said a little irritated. Tony stood up and started to exit the bar. "Where you going pop?" Terell asked.

"To The Palace to do some grown people things." Tony said as he left the bar area. "Don't drink the rest of my bottle and smoke that outside Terell, I'm serious."

Tony didn't really go to the Spot as much as he used to. It was like he out grew it when he gave Terell the business and he felt the Joint and the Palace were more of his flavor now.

As Tony left, Terell started to place the weed inside the joint paper. Elana sat down on Brian's lap and put her arms around him. She gave him a kiss on his cheek. It was evident that she missed him and you could see the love was strong between the two. Not seeing each other for nine months at a time made them miss each other more and the anticipation made the time that they did spend together that much better.

Mac rushed into the bar with urgency. "Hey man, some white boys just ran in the store and got us for some keys." Terell immediately got upset.

"What happened?" He asked glaring at Mac for the right answers.

"They got the coke and smacked Tim up, he sitting over there crying." Mac exclaimed he was looking at Elana sitting in Brian's lap which made her uncomfortable. Brian noticed the look but said nothing because his mind was more occupied with the situation at hand.

"I told you not to leave him there by alone!" Terell yelled.

"I ain't got no time to be baby sitting man, I'm the one who told you not to put him on." Mac responded, now his attention was back on Terell.

"He was supposed to keep track of the books, not man the store come on yall let's go see what's up." Elana stood up and watched as Terell and Mac ran out the bar area. Brian watched them run out until Terell called out for him. He looked at Elana for a second.

"I'll see you tonight at the carnival okay." Brian kissed her on the cheek and ran out to catch up with Terell and Mac.

<hr />

Timothy was sitting in Terell's dope spot in the back of a convenient store. He was balled up in a corner nervous, looking very pathetic. It was evident that he didn't belong in the game and the fact that Mac left him there wasn't the best decision which infuriated Terell because he cost Terell some money. Terell walked through the front as the clerk tried to get his attention. Terell knew he was giving him a heads up to what he already knew so he disregarded him and kept walking to the back.

As the door swung open Timothy started to spatter some gibberish like a child explaining themselves to a parent. Terell just watched him as he felt nothing but pity for the kid. Mac put him in a position where he was in way over his head but he also knew that somebody had to pay for this situation. Terell walked over to him and knelt down to his eye level.

"What happened Tim?" Terell asked attempting to sound sincere which wasn't working very well but Timothy was so distraught he couldn't tell the difference if Terell was genuinely concerned about him or not. He looked up at Terell with sheer fright and confusion in his eyes.

"It all happened so fast, some white boys came in here with guns. They threatened to kill me if I didn't tell them where the powder was so I told him." He started pointing at Mac. "I asked him not to leave me in here by myself. I seen them outside looking suspicious, but he had to go chase some girl." Timothy said almost crying.

Terell shot Mac a cold look. "You mean to tell me he told you about them, asked you to stay, and you left him here for some female. What's wrong with you man?" Terell focused his attention back to Timothy. "Look Tim, can you point them out to me again?" asked Terell.

"Yeah, I know they're going to be at the Carnival tonight too." Timothy said starting to calm himself down, he felt by giving Terell that information he saved his life.

"I guess I'm going to the carnival after all. Mac you better hope I get my keys back. Timothy I'm gonna pick you up in a couple of hours don't worry just point them out and everything will be alright."

Terell finally felt like he had the situation back in control. He handled it like his father, like a boss. If he would have went in there guns blazing then Timothy probably would of clammed up and forgot about the fact that they were going to the carnival or what they even looked like.

As they walked into the front Brian went to grab some soda and chips, he took them to the register and reached into his pocket.

"What are you doing Brian?" Terell asked. He assumed that Brian knew Terell used this place as his drug spot and he could run up the credit all he wanted.

"What's it look like, I'm getting some snacks, we still gonna smoke that weed right?" Brian loved weed, he wasn't much of a drinker but when it came to smoking he could do it with the best of them.

"You ain't gotta pay for nothin' in here man come on." Terell said as they kept walking out of the store.

"What's up wit' you boy, he don't know how this game work?" Mac asked. Brian wasn't going to let somebody who clearly messed up talk to him about the game so he was quick to respond to Mac's comment.

"At least I didn't leave a sniveling punk alone with a couple of keys to chase some chick." He stated as he got in the back seat.

Terell laughed which angered Mac even more. He knew he made a mistake but to have this kid come into town running his mouth, after having a girl he'd been chasing for years all in his lap talk trash to him made him very upset. Not to mention he was Terell's closest friend so while Terell was still breathing Brian was untouchable.

"Alright, keep running your mouth and you gonna get yo little ass whooped." Mac said, if he couldn't kill Brian he would beat him up he thought as they drove away.

Terell's mind was racing while they were in the car, he thought about Mac and questioned him as a right hand man. He definitely was a killer and a good man to have on his side but he was a wild card and the bottom line was that he couldn't trust him. Timothy was pretty much done because Mac put him in a spot to be a snitch and Terell couldn't chance it. Since Brian was back in town and he trusted him he thought about having Brian do his books and get another person to join his crew. He was about to recruit his next right-hand-man.

Kids of all ages were enjoying themselves at the Carnival. It was mostly African Americans but there were some white kids there also. It was 1983 and kids were going into each other's neighborhoods now. The older gangsters still didn't want to be in the other races territory though. All the lights made it look like a small Vegas and it was a lot of rides. Through all the positive energy and the fun going on nobody knew about the murderous intentions being plotted which made the carnival a dangerous place to be at. There was no quiet zone, anybody could do anything and get away with it. There was a river that ran underneath the carnival. There was a hill that went down by the entrance which wasn't a steep one so people could easily walk down it.

The carnival was lively and had the whole sky lit up as Terell, Brian and the rest of the crew stood by various rides and games with their eyes open. Brian and the rest of the guy's minds were in two different places. All Brian could think about was seeing Elana again while the rest were thinking about the situation that transpired earlier in the day. Timothy was the most obvious you could tell he was a nervous wreck. His eyes were peering through the crowd wide open, darting in every direction.

The two guys that robbed him were Irish, they had accents and looked rough. Terell was waiting for Timothy to spot them and then he planned on stalking them until he could catch them alone. He hoped they wouldn't spot him following them and make a run for it but he was willing to take that chance.

"Tim, you look like a junkie man, chill out." Mac said with a smirk on his face. The whole situation was amusing to him, how a person could be so weak and scared blew his mind away. Timothy saw the two who robbed them and nudged Terell.

"There they go." He whispered. Terell nudged Mac and motioned his head in the direction that the two Irish kids were walking in. "Chill out for a minute Brian, we 'bout to go handle this real quick." Terell said as the three started to follow them. Brian turned around and noticed the basketball game and decided to play it to occupy his time.

He gave the man who was running the game some money and got three balls to shoot for a stuffed animal. He didn't plan on keeping it but he wanted something to give Elana when she got to the carnival. Little did he know she was standing behind him watching him play the game. The first shot he just barely missed. As the man tossed him the second one he missed it terribly. He took his time with the third one and made the shot. He cracked a slight smile as he pondered which one she might like.

"We got a winner!" The man announced. "Which animal do you want?" Brian kept thinking and before he could answer Elana's voice caught him off guard again.

"The Tiger!" Brian turned around and felt his heart drop to his knees. She was the only person in the world who made him feel that way and he loved it.

The man grabbed the stuffed Tiger and handed it to her, she hugged it and wiped away a strand of hair that kept getting in her face. "Do you want to go for a walk?" Her voice still had him mesmerized after all these years, and he wasn't the only one. So many men tried to get her, using money to buy her love which didn't work. Some men even tried to play the friend role but after months of no sexual contact they eventually gave up but when it came to Brian it was like she had butterflies all over her body and even though she didn't give in to temptation there have been times where she had to catch herself.

"You don't want to go on a ride or anything?" Brian asked. He thought the point of the carnival was to do all the games and the rides or whatnot.

"Most men would try to get me alone. What game are you trying to play?" Her confidence was glowing all over her. She was right about his intentions but he didn't want to seem to eager. It was like the two of them were playing a game of cat and mouse.

"If I was like most men I assume you would treat me like most men. But I got some questions for you." Brian said.

"You don't have to get personal with me. I think you know me better than most people already." Elana said coolly.

Brian knew her, but it seemed like within this last year a lot of things have unfolded that he didn't know about and he was trying to find out everything that was going on with her so he wouldn't be blind-sided. Like the stares he received form Mac earlier when he was back at Tony's house, they were still on his mind. He wondered if there was something going on between the two of them.

Elana had a few questions of her own also, she know Terell's business and she didn't want to get caught up with anybody who had anything to do with the drug game. She didn't want to believe that Brian was involved but she feared that he could be involved even if it was indirectly. To her that could be the reason he moved back to town for good. The two of them needed to have a conversation before they could figure out where the relationship was headed.

.Brian and Elana walked down by the river. The cool breeze brought the right mix of warm and cool weather. It was peaceful and romantic. All that was missing was a violin player setting the mood. It was similar to Jimmy and Gina walking along that pier after they got married. Elana and Brian weren't exactly in love but they weren't far from it and the permanent move back for Brian definitely made it a strong possibility. Everything was different now, but in a good way. Both had questions they wanted to ask each other but a feeling of nervousness was between them.

Brian has his arm around her waist and she was holding her stuffed Tiger. His mind was racing because it wasn't a first date. She knew what he was going to school for and his dreams as well as Brian's background. He knew she wanted to be a entertainer in every since of the word and travel the world. They knew that the other had a good hearts, wanted kids, the things you normally get out of the way but now the tough part of the getting to know you stage was beginning.

"What's the deal with you and that Mac character?" Brian asked breaking the silence. He pretty much knew that she wasn't interested but he had to ask. Elana gave him a surprised look followed by a smile. She thought it was cute that he had a twinge of jealousy something she didn't think he had due to the fact that when he was in Atlanta he would always assure her that while they were apart if she felt the need to talk to somebody else wouldn't affect him that bad.

"There is nothing, wouldn't ever be nothing and hasn't ever been nothing between me and him. He has no goals but to be in the drug game which is what I don't want. Plus I see his type all the time there is nothing unique or different about him." Elana was kind of amused by the question but she had a couple of her own.

"So speaking of the drug game you're not involved in it are you because you know how I feel about that?" Brian stared at her for a second. Just like his question he was amused by hers and figured that she knew him better than that to even think he would be in the game. But at the same time she knew who his family was and the money that came along with it could tempt a saint.

"No, I won't lie I thought about it a couple of times you know, jumping in the family business if they needed me but I got a different set of goals and aspirations. But there is something you got to understand about me Elana, you can't ask me to pick between you and my family because that wouldn't be fair. I can promise you I won't get involved though." Brian stated, and it was enough for her to hear. She believed him and he was one of the only people in her life that didn't lie to her and the look in his eyes said nothing of the sort. His eyes had her hypnotized and she couldn't help but to trust him. Also, to her it would be like asking him to pick between her and her family.

"As long as you keep it honest with me Brian, please don't lie. Even if it's something you don't think I would like to hear at least give me a chance to change your mind about it instead of lying to me." They found a log on the beach and sat down on it Elana was still hugging her tiger, she got some sand stuck to her thigh and reached down to wipe it off with Brian eyes all over her and she recognized it, surprisingly the small non-contact gesture got her blood flowing a little bit. "Come here." She said in her best attempt at being seductive she hadn't had a lot of practice so it sounded kind of silly coming out of her mouth.

He leaned over and when they're lips touch fireworks exploded in a literal and metaphorical sense. Neither one had ever felt a feeling that they felt at that moment, they kept going with slight tongue being slipped into each other's mouths. Brian caressed her cheek and she couldn't bring herself to break away from him. Her body craved for his at that moment but her virtuous side still kept her composed. He wanted to grab her breast they were sitting perky and she wasn't wearing a bra but he knew it wasn't the time or the place to go to that step. She wanted him to caress her body also and there was no buts about it, if he would of made the attempt she wouldn't have stopped him.

Brian knew that with a woman like Elana less meant more. She wasn't a tease it was the way she was. He could tell that physically and mentally he had her right where he wanted her but he wanted that emotional connection which is what he was waiting to achieve. Once he had that he would be ready to connect with her and be one, his soul mate.

When their lips finally parted Elana was ready to get back to the carnival. "People might start to miss us, I told my friends I'd meet them here so are you ready to go back?" Brian's answer was no, but he was curious about what happened with Terell so he made his way back with Elana.

As the two started walking they began talking about small things, a little less personal and more comical. They were laughing together and the conversation went back to familiar territory. The two of them felt a little better about getting the serious topics out of the way. They still had more to talk about on that level but for the moment they were just enjoying each others company. Neither one of them could shake how the scenery made them feel. It was like some romantic movie that females watch all the time envisioning that their lives would play out that way, being swept off their feet by some prince charming type character

Terell watched the two Irish kids stop by a parked car which was parked on a hill, a perfect place to get them and take them off somewhere. Mac was already getting his gun out as they lurked in the shadows. Terell watched the glaze in Mac's eyes as he was anticipating the kill.

"Before you go all Tony Montana on me Mac we need information first. Tim you chill out here until we get 'em then follow us, don't think about running out on me." Terell ordered, but Tim thought he already done his job. His hands started shaking just at the sight of the two Irish kids and what was about to happen.

"I did my job Terell, what do you need me for?" He asked with a whine in his voice.

"Don't bitch up on me now man, just do what I say, come on Mac!" Terell exclaimed as him and Mac slowly approached the two Irish kids, they were instantly alarmed when they saw the two. Mac already had his gun out and pointed at them.

"Don't even think about running, just follow us down this hill now." Terell said calmly. They knew that Mac and Terell had the upper hand and all they could do was what they were told. Terell turned and looked back at Timothy then nodded his head in their direction Timothy reluctantly followed him.

"You should watch who you have in your crew, where's that one kid. It was funny to see him piss himself when we came in your spot." The bigger kid said, insulting Timothy was all he could do as Timothy caught up to them. Mac couldn't help but to laugh. The Irish kid had a gun on his back he was talking slick to a aspiring drug kingpin.

Once they reached the destination Terell slipped on his murder gloves just like his dad and made sure they seen him do it as a mental torture technique. He stared them down before getting to business.

"Where's my coke man?" Terell got straight to the point, he didn't think he would get an answer right away but regardless he was sending a message.

"We sold them to Henry Cartone" The smaller guy said. He wasn't as tough as his friend, he wasn't ready to die. He wasn't as pathetic as Timothy but he knew death was approaching and he was betting has last dollar that Terell might let him go if they say what he wanted also at this point he would rather deal with Henry Cartone then Terell.

"Shut up!" The bigger kid said. "He's lying we didn't sell him nothing." He knew Terell wasn't buying it but he made an attempt to get him to.

Terell was tired of playing around with them so he pointed the gun at the bigger kid first and shot him in the head. He pointed the gun at the other one next.

"So where you lying, did you sell them to Cartone or what?" Terell asked in a calm manner, he knew the answer he was just trying to get confirmation.

"Yeah, he's trying to get in the coke game." The kid responded.

"That doesn't make sense because he could have just went to his dad, don't lie to me!" Terell yelled.

"I swear to Christ, he bought them from us." The kid was now the one urinating on himself, he was sweating profusely before the next shot was fired killing him.

Terell put his gun up. Him and Mac grabbed the big kid and tossed him in the river that flew right behind them. They grabbed the other kid and followed with the same action. Terell then looked up at Timothy who was sitting down crying with his head between his knees, Terell nodded his head at Mac who walked behind Timothy without him noticing.

"Don't worry Tim okay, we got this mess taken care of. Not everybody is built for this life and it's obvious that you're not. I ain't gonna do anything to you just keep your mouth shut and we can act like this never happened." Terell was trying to soothe him but it wasn't working.

"But it did." Timothy sobbed, I just seen two people get killed Terell how can I live with that." Timothy felt Mac's presence and caught him off guard knocking the gun out of his hand, and running for his life. He didn't get far before Terell shot him in the back dropping him on his stomach.

Terell ran up to his body and shot him one more time in the back of his head killing him. Mac picked his gun up and ran up to Terell to help him throw Timothy in the river with the other two. After they completed the plan Mac wiped the sweat from his brow.

"He had some fight in him after all." Mac said between breaths.

"Come on let's get back up to the carnival so we can make sure we're seen there." Terell stated as the two began walking in the direction that they came down in.

The calm river had a strong flare to it. Water became murky and reddish green. It was filled with three bodies with bullet holes. While everybody was having a good time above the riverside death was filling the air down by the riverside

Terell and Mac were standing by a hot dog cart with two females discussing their next move. The two females were very intoxicated and not paying any attention to them or what they're talking about. Terell's mind was still wondering why Henry Cartone would be competing with his father for business but Mac's mind was occupied with sex like it normally is.

"He must be trying to move in on my territory." Said Terell. He watched and waited for Mac's opinion but noticed he wasn't paying attention. "Are you listening to me?" Mac's lack of interest about serious business was irritating him. "You know what man, you like the women more than you like the money and that's your problem." Terell said. Just like Tony did Eric back in the day Terell found himself having to instruct Mac how to act when it came to the business they were in. Terell had his mind made up that Henry would be a problem, he sensed that a war was coming, a decade year old war that his father squashed a couple of years ago.

"Where your cousin at man?" Mac said breaking his silence, he had been thinking about her all night and it never occurred to him that she could be remotely interested in Brian. Sure he saw her in his lap earlier but he was so cocky that he felt like if he couldn't get no action nobody else couldn't get any either.

"You need to give up on that man, she's been on Brian for years and now that he's back for good there's no way your going to get next to her. What you need to do is get your mind ready for Cartone." Terell stated trying to get his soldier's mind back in the battle. "We need some more muscle, do you got anybody in mind?" Terell was getting upset with Mac and more and more he started second guessing his ability to be his lieutenant which was an important position in his camp. His father told him time and time how important Eric was to him before he got killed and he was stuck with a silly cat like Mac.

"I can hit the streets and recruit for you. But your going to have to make the final decisions. What about the books though, Timothy ain't no longer here?" Mac inquired.

"Brian can handle that temporarily until we find somebody else." Terell said with his mind still occupied with what Henry had up his sleeve.

"Don't get him involved T, he's just another Timothy." Mac was starting to get mad about the relationship Terell and Brian had and it was starting to show in his demeanor which bothered Terell. No matter what Mac and him been through Brian was way more important to him and he wasn't going to put up with much more insults from Mac about Brian. Especially because he was jealous over Elana, in Terell's eyes that was something that made Mac look extremely weak.

One of the females, who was a chocolate thick young lady and was very pretty came over and wrapped her arms around Terell. He hugged her back enough to show her some attention but he wasn't all the way focused on her because his money motivated mind frame was being threatened at the moment. He still showed her attention though giving her soft kisses on her cheek and neck.

Mac's girl was looking bored but that didn't matter to him. She had the complete eighties girl look popping her bubble gum with the Whitney Houston bun in her hair. She was an average girl and his mind was on the A plus chick that he'd been chasing.

It's not necessarily Elana herself that he's attracted to it's the fact that she holds out on him. If he ever got in her pants the thrill would be gone which is how dudes like him operate. When a woman can see through that and resist the appearance and the money then his plan seems to fall into the void category. Mac watched Terell's display of affection and thought about what Terell had just said to him.

"Now who's caught up in the women?" He asked with a playful smirk on his face.

"You know what Mac, I'm not gonna be standing here looking pretty like I am and you not paying any attention to me, it's disrespectful." The girl said as she rolled her eyes with her long eye lashes and mocha skin she was actually gorgeous if she wasn't so dolled up.

"Just chill baby, and be glad your option number two, alright." Mac said without any eye contact with the young lady. As he kept looking for Elana he seen two figures approaching in the distance and at his dismay he saw his trophy with another man's arms wrapped around her. He kept his emotions in check but as the figures got clear his composure started to decrease.

As Elana and Brian walked up to the group they immediately felt the heat coming from Mac which made the vibe awkward. Terell had stopped thinking about the situation with Cartone and found his mind one hundred and ten percent involved in the young lady he was with, he only turned his head away from her to acknowledge their presence.

"What's up bro, is everything okay with you?" Brian asked, Terell wished Brian wouldn't of brought that up because he just snapped out of feud mode but he knew Brian was just worried.

"Yeah man, it's nothing that we can't take care of, where were you guys at?" Terell asked seeing the huge smile on his cousin's face and the public display of affection something he had never seen from her before.

"Don't worry about all that, you don't tell me your business so we don't have to tell you ours." Elana said with a smile on her face. Elana and Terell had the kind of relationship where they often joked around with each other but it was something different about his cousin that he recognized and liked and nothing could make him happier that it was Brian who brought that side of her out, a more loose side.

"What did you do to my cousin Brian? She talking different, you only been back here for a day." Terell said starting to focus back on his lady for the moment. Mac watched the whole thing sickened, he couldn't believe what he was seeing and his lady friend was noticing the tension and was at her boiling point.

"If you keep gawking at her go 'head and try your luck, but it looks like she's already taken. I got better things to do like enjoy the carnival, I'll see you guys later." The girl stormed off and Mac didn't even chase her. Terell watched her walk off and then looked back at Mac and knew what was about to come next.

"Why don't you stop cuffing her man." Mac said while he approached Elana, just feeling his presence come close to her made her shiver in a negative way. Brian didn't know what to do, either stop him in his tracks or let Elana handle herself. He choose to let her handle it because no matter what Mac tried to do him or Terell wouldn't let the situation go to far.

"Look Mac, I've told you time after time, you're not my type and me and Brian are getting to know each other. Don't walk up on me, or try to talk to me in that way, do me a favor and show some respect which is something you could never do." Elana spoke to him sternly. She was fed up with him and was tired of explaining the same thing over and over again.

Mac just stood there stunned. "You see I already had something lined up for later and she's gone because of you. So you're just going to leave me hanging like that." Mac was pleading at this point, and Terell found the situation funny.

"Bye guys. Can you walk me home Brian?" Elana asked still frustrated with what just transpired.

"Yeah." stated Brian. As they walked off Mac called to them.

"Yeah, walk her home Brian!" Brian ignored Mac, to him he was acting silly and finally realized that he had lost. The girl choose him and that's all that mattered.

Terell just stared at Mac while his girl was in his ear getting him to jump on the exit train with her. He was all packed and ready to go.

"See you tomorrow man we need to get to business, I'm calling you early in the mourning." Terell stated as he walked off with his girl. Mac put on his game face because he was back on the prowl for a woman.

Brian and Elana were tired and done with drama for the day but they weren't done as they were exiting the carnival they ran to her brother Giovanni and his cousin Henry Cartone along with the other two members of their crew Phil and Sonny.

Elana's heart dropped she felt like taking Brian by the hand walking right pass them but that was her brother and cousin so she knew they would stop her. How much worse could the day get she thought to herself. She felt them approaching and all eyes were on her.

Just like Mac, Sonny had an eye for her but he had no respect for black people in general so when he approached her he would border-line disrespect her culture which turned her off completely.

Giovanni stared at Brian but remained silent. It was weird for them to see each other since it had been so long because every time Brian came back for the summer he hadn't crossed paths with Giovanni. Henry's first thought was maybe it was some kind of problem between the two but he brushed that off because he didn't sense any hatred, it was something else there.

"Is there a problem cousin?" Henry asked Giovanni. "Because if there is we can take care of it for you." Henry started to approach Brian but Elana stepped in front of him.

"We were just leaving Henry, they haven't seen each other in some time, that's all it is right?" Elana's question was more directed to her brother than Brian.

"Yeah, I remember you, you used to be around when we were little, didn't my uncle Tony have something to do with your dad getting killed?" Brian was upset that he would bring that up, but to avoid any conflict he chose to keep his mouth shut on the topic.

"Something like that." He took his eyes off of Giovanni but could still feel him staring at him.

"Hey Marie! Why don't you come hang out with us and call some of your friends up. I know you must have at least a couple of white ones." Henry said it more as an order than a question. Elana had no interest so she rolled her eyes at Henry and grabbed Brian the hand. The two of them continued their walk as the small crew watched them for a minute.

Sonny tapped Giovanni on the shoulder insinuating that he wasn't doing a very good job hooking him up with his sister, according to them if he told her to date one of his friends it should be no questions asked. Her father wasn't around anymore so it was his job to make sure she did what he told her, or how they saw it keep her away from the black crowd.

"Why is it that your sister acts so black?" Sonny asked. "Is it that you're pretending to be one of us or is it that she's pretending to be one of them." Giovanni didn't appreciate what Sonny was getting at but he was used to their humor about him being mixed. Henry kept them from getting to far out of line but deep down in his heart he agreed with them but he saw Cartone blood before anything.

Henry felt about Giovanni the same way Terell felt about Brian, even though they were the same age he felt like he needed to protect him. The only difference was Giovanni was cut out to be a gangster and Henry had a spot for him in his plans for the drug game. On the other hand Brian wasn't so Terell wanted to keep him away from it by any means necessary.

When Brian and Elana arrived to her house it was completely different. What once was a unique blend of African American and Italian cultures turned into a bland space with room, sort of like the study at the Cartone mansion. Nevertheless when Elana got home she automatically felt relief. What was supposed to be a good day turned out to be confrontational and stressful. Brian walked in the house and slightly remembered it. He had been there a couple of times as a kid and remembered the chess set that sat in the corner of the living room. Elana was walking around the house making herself comfortable she took her shoes off and went into the kitchen and opened the freezer.

"You can have a seat." It was her first time being a hostess so she was nervous but she didn't let it show. Brian walked over to the couch and sat down he rubbed his hands together still looking around the home waiting for her to come back and sit down. In a few moments she was coming into the living room with a bowl of ice cream in her hand, the spoon in the middle of the top scoop as she sighed when her behind hit the couch. She scrounged her legs up on the couch and stared at Brian for a second.

"Who were those guys with your brother?" Brian asked. He didn't like the looks he was getting from them and wondered if he was going to have some problems in the near future. "The one with the short hair was looking at me the same way Mac was, it's like your gonna have me fighting everybody in the neighborhood over you girl." Brian joked.

Elana took a bite of her ice cream and rubbed her foot. "Sonny has been liking me forever but he's a racist and you know how I feel about that. I'm tired of being the object of every man's admiration. I guess I better get used to it if I'm going to live out my dream of a entertainer." Brian nodded his head in agreement. "If that's what you want to do you're gonna have to get used to the spotlight." He stated. He had to keep his mind from undressing her to keep up with their conversation he still couldn't get that kiss out of his mind.

"Could you handle having a girlfriend who wants to be an actress or a singer?" She asked as she kept eating her ice cream.

"Sure, you aren't the only one with dreams, I would be focused on my goals and to have somebody who got a full plate may actually be helpful for me to focus on what I gotta do with my dreams." Brian could feel the sexual tension in the air just like it was at the carnival but this time they were alone in her house with her bedroom right around the corner.

Elana finished off her ice cream and stood up her backside jiggled in her dress and when she walked Brian bit down on his lip just trying to keep his manhood tamed. He started sweating a little bit and telling his mind to stop thinking about anything sexual. His mind went into coach mode and his limbs were his players.

This time when she came back into the living room to sit down she sat down halfway of the distance she was away from him. She enjoyed her little sexual game she was playing. She wasn't a tease usually but she thought the way he was keeping himself in check was admirable and she wanted to see how far she could take it before he would turn into every other man and try to pull some kind of seduction move, like a massage or foot rub, she had heard it all before.

"So your mom decided not to move after all these years?" Brian asked trying to change the subject.

"Yeah after the robber came and killed my father, I tried to get her to move but she wouldn't listen." Brian knew the truth about what happened but he had no clue that Elana didn't know that her uncle killed her father and he wasn't going to say anything, even though he had to catch himself.

"What was my brother talking about, my uncle Tony killed your dad?" She asked confused and he felt sorry for her because nobody let her in on any of the family drama but this question he couldn't avoid so he felt like he should tell her the story even though he hated to talk about it.

"This is a sore subject for me Elana, I really don't want to talk about it." He tried to get her to leave it alone but those green eyes of hers had him mesmerized. He was starting to second guess being with her, he feared she might have a way of getting him wrapped around her finger because she was already doing it.

"It was that day when we built that clubhouse in Terell's backyard and your dad came to pick up you and your brother." Elana remembered that day and thought about Brian's dad dying the same day she was at her Uncle's house. She wanted to speak but she let him finish. "My dad came over and got drunk and high and just started beatin' me like he normally did. Tony pulled his gun out and gave him his final warning because he was tired of it. My dad beat me for no reason besides that I was being taught to be better than him. You could call it jealousy but to me it was pure hatred and to be honest I'm not mad he's dead." Elana was trying her hardest to not put her opinion in and letting Brian finish but it was eating at her to speak, but against her judgment she allowed him to proceed.

"So Tony told him that if he hit me again he would shoot him and the next thing my father did was started slapping me and Tony shot him." Brian's face remained stone cold frozen, Elana had never seen him look so blank and careless, it seemed to her like Brian felt like his father got what he deserved and she was right about that. She hugged Brian for a couple of seconds before releasing him.

"Murder is justifiable, only if it's self-defense. I love my Uncle Tony but what he did was wrong and until you confront him about killing your father it will haunt you." Elana said. But she could see there was no reaching him and that topic was hard for Brian to deal with. She felt bad just bringing it up.

Elana kept watching him look straight ahead and figured out a way to get his spirit's back up which was planting another kiss on him. Those same sparks flew again when their lips touched and instantly Brian forgot about his father. She started to lean her body back on the couch cushion as she guided his hand to explore parts of her body starting with her thigh and then the outline of her curves.

Brian allowed her to guide his hand instead of taking control because he felt that Elana liked having it until she gave it away and he would be able to tell when she would do that. He broke the kiss with her lips and started to kiss her jaw line and the back of her earlobe.

Her moan was music to his ears and this was the first time she felt pure bliss, waves went throughout her body and she hadn't felt anything yet. She knew it wouldn't happen tonight but she was experiencing a partial feeling of euphoria and even though Brian was sexually experienced he hadn't felt anything like he was feeling at that moment either.

The two stopped and looked at each other. The silence set back in and both of them were feeling that it was time for him to leave, but neither were making the attempt to bring it up.

The door opened and Gina came in and looked at the two of them in shock. She didn't see any red flags of inappropriate behavior but the fact that Elana never brought anybody home let alone a male through her for a loop. After her initial shock she recognized who it was and felt some relief that it was somebody who she knew and actually liked. Gina knew about Brian because Tony spoke so highly of him and in a way he reminded her of Jimmy. His intelligence and compassion for people along with his ability not place judgment on people he cared about were all traits of Jimmy that she cherished.

"Hi Ms. Cartone." Brian started, he was a little embarrassed. He stood up and walked over to greet her seeing as though she still was coming up with words to say to him.

"Hi Brian, I didn't know you were in town, how long are you staying for?" She questioned expecting to hear him say just a couple of months like he did every summer." Gina was staring a hole through his head as if she was trying to read his mind, but Brian remained eye contact and kept his composure.

"I'm back for good, I'm finishing my senior year and going to USC to study journalism. I want to write about all the injustice and unfair treatment going on in the world today." He said in his best save the world mentality voice.

"Okay, well it was good to see you." Gina said and Brian picked up on her rushing him out of the house so he started to walked out of the door quickly.

"Yes mam, you guys have a good night I'll call you later Elana." As Brian left Gina instantly went to her daughter's side who had stood up and went into the kitchen dreading the talk she was about to have with her mother.

"We weren't doing anything mom. Just talking." Elana stated assuring her mother that she was still a virgin but she knew her mother was worried that Elana's sudden interest in boys was happening to fast. Also Gina knew first hand that being involved with Brian would bring nothing but hurt and pain, just like her and Jimmy.

"Don't get to close and try to learn from my mistakes. I have no reason not to trust you and you have no reason not to listen to me, stay away from him!" It was like Gina was demanding her but it was no point Elana was on her way to being head over heels in love with Brian.

Tommy Cartone sat in the dining room of the Cartone mansion. The death of his father hit him pretty hard and he was strongly considering getting out of the game. Joining him for a meal was Charlie who was his Uncle. Charlie had flew in from Miami when he found out about the death of Paul and wanted to be around his family.

Tommy rested his head in his hands discussing the possibilities of who murdered his dad and he was still convinced that the Delena family had something to do with it. Over the years the quarrel between them hadn't gotten any better and Tommy was set on revenge. The possibility of Tony hitting Paul wasn't out of his mind but he knew that Tony and Larry were having issues over the black neighborhoods so the likelihood of Tony coming after his father a few years later didn't make any sense to him. Charlie wasn't really helping him because he was sent to smooth things over. The Cartone family still were good earners for the mob and they could still fly under the radar of police which kept things quiet.

"I'm telling you Tommy this cowboy is back to his old tricks. Carlo's people assured me that they had nothing to do with Paul getting murdered." Charlie said between bites of spaghetti.

Larry entered the room obviously upset. He stormed in like he owned the place. Tommy wasn't in the mode to deal with him but he at least had to hear him out because of their business arrangement.

"I thought you guys had my back Cartone, Tony's been retired but his son is still making some major moves on my streets!" Larry exclaimed. His tone was a lot different then the first time he came to get spotted keys to get in the game.

"What do I care about his kid, if you couldn't handle him that's on you, I did my part of our arrangement and have been for years. Besides, me and my family is concerned it might be about time to quit this life." Tommy was waiting for an objection from Charlie but got none which struck him as odd because if he cared about the Cartone family he would know that drugs were their source of revenue.

"It was Tony that hit your old man, now he's too crafty for me to get to myself but if we team up we can get him." Larry was almost shouting but remained calm enough to be respectful, he got no response out of Tommy which irritated him. His plan to get the Cartone's and Tony to go to war wasn't working and he was wracking his brain to figure something before Tony would hit him.

"Look Larry, this is your fight, I'm dealing with something else right now. You and Tony can can try and kill each other it's what you blacks do anyway. If you were smart you would divide up the territory so everybody can eat but you're too greedy to do that. Leave me out of it. You still got the connect from us but once I decide if I'm out your going to have to figure out something else." Charlie stopped eating his food and looked up at Tommy. He listened and caught on to Larry's idea which was similar to his own.

"Wait nephew, he has a point. Tony is the most logical and he has the most to gain from Pauly's death, maybe we should hit him." Charlie said and then instantly continued eating.

"I'm not jumping to any conclusions, until I feel that Carlo Delena had nothing to do with my father dying, I'm not doing anything. Do both of you understand that? Larry can you please . . . ."

Before Tommy could finish his thought Henry, Giovanni and the rest of his crew stormed in the room.

"Pop I need to talk to you, it's important!" Henry said with a steep sense of urgency. He was holding the bag with the two keys of coke that he bought from the Irish kids that robbed Terell.

"What now? Can't you see I'm busy kid, this is gonna have to wait a minute." Tommy said.

Henry emptied the contents of the bag on the table and the men in the room looked at him with confused looks on their faces. For all they knew Henry had no interest in the drug game and now he busts in like he's some kind of kingpin.

"Where did you get this from Henry?" Tommy asked with a look of concern on his face, he knew Henry wasn't no scholar but he didn't want this life for his son especially since he was thinking about retiring. Henry gave him a look of innocence.

"Just some black kid, so what, I thought this would prove to you how serious I am and I don't need any handouts to take over the business." Henry thought his father would be proud of him and in a way Tommy was. If Henry was determined to walk in the footsteps of his father and grandfather he was going about it the right way. Not only did he get it himself, he asked for permission to sell it, he was proud of his son.

"You two, get out of my house." Tommy said coldly pointing at Phil and Sonny, they left quickly without saying a word. "You and Giovanni sit down for a second. So you're doing this too nephew?" Tommy's eyes made Giovanni a little uncomfortable but he kept staring at his Uncle nodding his head.

"I'm with Henry, if this is what he decides to do I got his back." Giovanni said noticing that Tommy was believing him. In his heart he had no intention on getting in the game but he also had no intentions on school which he had dropped out of years ago. He did wonder what he would do with his life and if this was his path he would rather be with his family then by himself.

"You know your mother can't find out about this she'll wack me out herself if she found out so don't say anything to her about it, okay." Giovanni nodded his head, he didn't want his mother to know just like Tommy didn't.

"So do I got your permission or what pop?" Henry asked anxiously.

"Yeah, you just made up my mind for me, I'm out this business and if you want to keep the Cartone name going it's all yours. I'll help you out a little bit, but this is all on you now son." Tommy was proud, Henry stood to his feet and he embraced his son.

Larry was enraged not only couldn't he get Tony out of the way but right as Tommy was planning on quitting his son hops in the game and he had the Cartone name to back him so instead of no competition now it was back at two competitors. Larry shook his head as Henry and Giovanni walked out of the office.

"You know he had to rob Tony's son, you better watch out for that." Larry said, Tommy didn't listen to Larry's warning it could just be him running his mouth.

"Seems like you're caught up in child's play Larry, you got kids taking you off your game what are you going to do next maybe babysitting, I'm surprised you've lasted this long." Tommy and Charlie started laughing at Tommy's joke which upset Larry even more. Larry just stared at them while they laughed, he was coming up with an idea, he was gonna take care of Terell first and then next was gonna be Henry Cartone and then he was going to run the game and take out Tommy Cartone the last one left.

As Larry stormed out of the office Charlie and Tommy kept laughing

"Do you want a drink Uncle Charlie" Tommy asked between chuckles, Charlie was laughing to hard to respond so he just nodded, Tommy made both of them a drink and sat down.

Terell stood in the middle of a basketball court in the neighborhood where his father grew up along with Mac. Even though he lived out in a nicer part of town he spent more time in the hood then his father. It was in him, the smell of it captured him. He felt it was important to know these nickel and dime dealers who were developing aspirations to take his spot so he could crush their hopes before they started. He rested his head and his valuables were kept out at his dad's house but you could always find him in the ghetto. Even on special occasions he was never in The Joint or The Palace he was always at The Spot with the hustlers and gangsters.

It's was a hot sunny day. Terell and Mac got a prospect to add to their crew. His name was Ricky and he just got out of the penetinutary a few months ago for manslaughter. Terell had his shirt off and he was sweating profusely from just finishing a basketball game. He watched a couple of junkies fighting over a needle was laughing at them. Ricky heard about Terell's reputation but never met him. He knew Mac for a long time and understood what he was getting into.

"So Mac explained to you what I do right? I'm not like these niggas out here." Terell waited for his response and seen that if Ricky was impressed he didn't let him know. Terell was trying to read him but he couldn't off first impressions which was usually a good sign. He liked Ricky's confidence and rough exterior, he reminded him of Mac but he didn't run his mouth as much.

"These niggas out here cooking up this shit taking all these chances for pennies ain't gonna move up in the world, you're older than me so you know. I need somebody who's trying to get his hands on some serious money and get mixed up with the kingpins in the game." Ricky was listening to every word Terell said and even though he didn't show it he was extremely impressed. He heard about Tony and about how he didn't hand Terell anything. He respected how Terell actually put work in to get to his spot.

Ricky was twenty-one years old and he hadn't met anybody with the connections like Terell had. Once Mac came to him asking him to get down he already knew he would be in on it. Terell seen his make-up and heard the stories. He knew that Ricky would be his muscle and if needed Ricky would be the one to get troops ready.

"So what's it gonna be, we don't have to discuss money because I'm gonna offer you more money you ever seen in your life." Terell waited for his answer and got a head nod which was all he expected from Ricky. With that out the way he turned around and got back to the basketball game at hand.

Terell was watching a game wrap up where some big mouth cat was hitting a jump shot over Mac to win the game. You could tell he was one of those ballers that could have played college and went pro if he had his head on straight because he was that good. He got caught up in smoking weed, not keeping up with school and sex to loose track of his main goal which should have been basketball.

"I told yall I'm the best, if I liked school I'd be in college right now on my way to the league!" The baller boasted. He looked around and seen that nobody was impressed. "Oh what! Any doubters, well I know some of yall got some money out here, put yo money where yo mouth is then." He started peeling off hundreds from a fat wad of cash from his pocket.

Terell turned to Ricky as he spoke. "Do you see this fool man, I'm 'bout to take his money." Terell said confidently.

"Do what you do man." Ricky said coolly as he walked to the sideline and watched the perimeter already doing his job. As the trash talking started between Terell and the baller everybody came to watch the event. When gambling was going on especially in street ball, it was very entertaining. Emotions would flare and attitudes would jump out of this world.

"Give me the ball! How we playin' sweetheart?" Terell asked.

"After every shot made we drop another hundred in the pot. If you miss and I make it's mine." The baller said as he was waiting for some kind of fear from Terell.

Terell chuckled to himself as he got the ball in his hands and went behind the three point line which was run over and barely visible. He took a shot on a ripped net and it went in not toughing the rim, he kept his hand up in a shooter's position showing his form. He remained silent and walked over to the side. The baller walked over to the same spot and with the same swagger if not more made the shot not hitting the rim and pulled another hundred out of his pocket.

"Come on money bags put another hundred in the pot man." Terell dropped another hundred and noticed a car pulling up slowly. It made his focus slow down but he ignored it which was something any amount of money would do rather it was four hundred or four thousand dollars. He dribbled the ball, took the shot and missed it. He cringed his face up in disappointment but still had hope that his opponent would miss and the game would keep going.

"Too bad man, money gone once I hit this." The baller said seriously. As he aimed for the shot his body jerked as bullets filled his chest up.

Three black teenagers ran on the court shooting wildly. Terell ducked down and ran for cover pulling his gun out of the back part of his jeans. He turned around and started shooting back. He noticed that Ricky was already standing strong letting off shots from his gun hitting one of the shooters. The gun fight continued as everybody who didn't have a gun dispersed. Mac, Terell along with Ricky were standing firm and not backing down, they were shooting precisely with good aim hitting two of the gunmen and dropping them to the ground. The third gunman shot Mac in his leg as he dropped and grabbed his leg, the gunman received a flurry of stinging hot bullets from Terell and Ricky.

"Get your whip!" Terell ordered Ricky. He went over to Mac and tried to get him to his feet. "Come on man, we gotta get you to the hospital." Mac winced in pain as he placed his arm around Terell and hobbled on one foot to the door that led to the basketball court. Ricky had the car parked and the passenger door open. He hopped out and opened the back door as Terell placed Mac in the back seat. Terell slammed the door shut and got in the passenger seat as Ricky sped off.

It was a quiet ride to the hospital. Mac was slightly groaning while Terell was thinking about the situation. Normally when people get shot they cry and curse but Mac was a soldier and he took it in stride. Once they reached the Emergency room the doctors immediately took Mac away and Terell and Ricky sat down in the waiting room. There is always a certain feeling in a hospital room, a lot of people don't like them it could be because of all the deaths that occur in them. Terell didn't care he'd been in the hospital and put people in the hospital but not Mac.

"You weren't playing when you said this game was viscous. If it's like this everyday I'm wearing a bullet proof vest with me everywhere I go." Ricky said. It was his first day on the job and he was already involved in a gun fight. Terell just looked at him. His mind was occupied about figuring out who planned the hit. It was sloppy and the gunmen were a bunch of young punks who used some twenty-two's instead of fully automatic weapons. If they were to use those big guns then they would all be dead.

Tony arrived with Leroy and Brian. He found Terell and Ricky waiting in the room looking stressed.

"How's he doing?" Tony asked. He could see his son was worried but he wondered if it was about Mac or about the hit itself. This was the first time Terell had experience this kind of adversity in the drug game.

"They said he's gonna pull through but he took it like a man. He lost a lot of blood pop but he'll make it and be back to running his mouth like he's known for." Terell cracked a slight smile even though Mac worked his nerves almost every second he's around him, he had love for him. "I'm trying to figure out who would do this. It was sloppy and they had little punk ass guns." Terell stared at his father for advice.

Tony sat down and thought hard about the situation, it had been some years since he'd been in war time mode, after he killed Mario the war beast lost some savageness. He wanted to rule Larry out but then again he knew it could be a major insult to Larry's ego to have a kid come in this game and be on his level financially.

Then there was Tommy Cartone, he could have some ill feelings about Paul's death and wanting to get to Tony through Terell which made sense but wasn't his style. On the other hand it wouldn't surprise him if Tommy wanted to finish off the war he started ten years ago.

Or it could be somebody trying to make a name for them selves like he did with Vincent, there were too many options to choose from.

Terell had a totally different way of thinking, and Tony could see it in his son's eyes. To him it was kill all of them, he had the Michael Corleone idea from the Godfather. His eyes were bloodshot red and the anger ran so rugged through his body that he got goose bumps.

"Calm down son, I see where your mind is going and don't go there." Tony said, he was starting to see that Terell's anger would be his demise. Once somebody is tested that's when you find out if they're ready to be the man in the business that they were involved in. Tony remained calm even when he was about to kill and that's what made him have longevity in the coke game before he gave the reigns over to Terell.

"Mac is laid up in there with a bullet wound and you want me to calm down!" Terell yelled. He hopped up out of his chair and was almost in his father's face. People in the hospital started to stare at them and when he felt their gazes on him he started to mellow out. Terell sat back down with both hands in his head in a thinking position.

"So what are you gonna do now?" Brian asked. He was getting things going with Elana and didn't want nothing to start between Terell and the Cartone family. He didn't know everything but he knew a little something about these recent events.

"Stay out of this college boy, don't worry . . ." Before Terell could finish his statement Tony interrupted him. "Who is he?" he asked pointing at Ricky.

Terell was so wrapped up in the altercation that he failed to introduce Ricky to his father which was a sign of disrespect in Tony's eyes. A thing so small as that kept chopping at Tony's confidence in his son to handle this issue but he pushed it to the back of his mind.

"Sorry pop, this is Ricky he's apart of my crew, this is his first day on the job and he smoked a couple of cats already. He had my back out there." Terell appreciated Ricky's quick draw and no fear mentality, Mac was right about him and he was glad that he had him on the team.

"Back to this hit, I think it was Larry, it makes the most since to me. He don't have no connect on big guns that's why he couldn't bring fully automatics and it was in the hood. If it was Cartone he would came blastin' with the real deal like he did me when he shot The Spot up." Tony said as he sat back and waited for what Terell would have to say about his interpretation of the situation.

"That makes since but I think we should hit all of them just in case. I found out that Henry Cartone is getting in the game, he bought the two keys from the white boys who robbed me. So he gotta go too."

"But you're not for sure if he did anything." Brian said trying to come with a rebuttal.

"I told you to stay out of this Brian." Terell snapped, he wasn't mad at him, he was just frustrated and to him there was no reason for Brian to even be talking.

"Let's just take this slow." Tony wanted to let it all play out. Terell could be right because of the information he just gave him about Henry but he wanted to see first. He felt like if he didn't rush and kill Vinny then Jimmy would still be alive so since then he carefully plotted all of his moves. He was trying to teach his son the same lesson but he was so hot headed.

"Either you scared of Tommy Cartone or you trying to get a piece of his sister's pie, or something!" Now Terell was being full blown disrespectful and if they weren't in a public place Tony would have beat some respect back into his son but he remained calm and allowed his son to speak his mind. He had no feelings for Gina and fear has never been in his vocabulary so he did entertain his son's thoughts furthermore he knew Terell was trying to provoke him.

"Shut up and listen to me! I said just wait, I'm gonna take care of Larry and we'll figure out what to do about the Cartone's all of them."

"Come on pop let me off him!" Terell exploded jumping out of his chair. He achieved glances and stares from the people in the hospital area which calmed him down. Tony nodded his head at Leroy and he stood up to leave.

"No, just chill out and listen to what I said don't do nothin' until I tell you." Tony stated as him and Leroy walked out of the area. Terell sat back down in the same position and he noticed Brian looking at him. He went over to Brian and sat down next to him. He ran his hand over Brian's head attempting to comfort him because he knew he had been harsh on him.

"Sorry man, I just don't want you to worry about this." Terell could see the concern in Brian's face and he knew exactly why, because of Elana. He knew what was coming and he knew what could come of it which was the same thing that happened to his Uncle getting caught between the woman he loved and his family.

Henry jumped and the coke game quickly and started running even faster. His ruthless demeanor and quick temper made everybody get the message that the Cartone family was back. His father, especially in his later years of running the drug game had became more passionate but Henry was far from that. He was a young Tommy but not as calm similar to Terell. Giovanni watched his cousin and at times was his voice of reason but he couldn't always control Henry.

Phil was in charge of the books and the distribution of money to the soldiers that the Cartone family had lined up. They were happy that Henry was in charge because most of them were saying that Tommy had went soft. Sonny was in charge of setting up the deals with buyers and he was a pro at his job, his cunning mannerism was on point and perfect for the coke game.

The Cartone family was more organized than ever and they were turning heads even the Mob boss's were recognizing that Henry was a good earner like his grandfather. He maintained the ability to keep below the radar of the feds by not being to greedy. In the eyes of the big boys the Cartone family was a myth and maintained a myth because of the way they conducted business. Anybody who thought about snitching was threatened with the loss of their life and if that didn't work they were offered so much cash that their family could be set for life. If the person was really protected they would break themselves to bribe them to keep freedom. Business was going good but on this particular night another issue was addressed.

Henry and his crew were sitting in the basement of the Cartone home counting money. There were all kinds of pipes and a small area where they set up shop at. It wasn't the most cozy spot but something about it made it feel like his own place. He wasn't the only one that hated being down there but he was calling the shots. All the twenties, fifties and hundreds that sat on the table had eyes and it was staring it them with a gleam. When you get to a certain level of success you feel untouchable in the lifestyle of a gangster and Sonny had a little much to drink. His jealousy of Giovanni got the best of him on that particular occasion.

"Hey Vanni, when are you gonna get me a date with that sister of yours, I'm starting to get offended." Sonny spat, he knew what he was doing Elana was just a way to get under his skin. Giovanni also knew what this was about, Sonny had never liked him and he was attracted to Elana but he would use that as a way to start an issue with him. Sonny also knew that Henry shared the same chauvinist beliefs. Because Giovanni was her brother he should make her go out with his friend if he asked.

"Yeah cousin, he's been asking for months and you still haven't done it, it kind of bothers me she's always hanging out with those niggers." Henry was also drunk and he knew he was talking about Giovanni's other side of his family but he didn't care,

"She doesn't like you man, just like she don't like half of the guys in L.A. What do you want from me? She's gonna be her and that's it." Giovanni was getting irritated and it was blatant.

"Grow a pair of balls for starters." Sonny said taunting him. The comment caused Phil and Henry to laugh. Giovanni wasn't amused and he started to stare Sonny down as if he was going to punch him in the face. "What are you gonna do, you're looking at me like your gonna do something." Sonny said.

"Come on guys count the money, we got thousands of dollars here and you're arguing over some broad, no disrespect intended." Phil said as the voice of reason he didn't understand what the bickering back and forth was all about everybody should have been estatic the way he saw it.

"This ain't about my sister, there's something else this prick has been wanting to say to me, come on Sonny, you're all liquored up so speak your mind." Now Giovanni was the one playing the mind games and Sonny was playing right into his hand.

"You're right, as far as I'm concerned you're just a nigger who got lucky to be born a Cartone. If it wasn't for Henry you would have been dead a long time ago." Sonny was just getting started.

"Easy Sonny." Henry interrupted but it was too late Giovanni's plan was working.

"You and your sister act like you're something special at least she can be who she is but you slick you're hair back, you talk like us, walk like us, you mess with white broads, but your not Italian." Sonny stood up and staggered slightly and his words were slurring.

"Your whole family is a bunch of fakes, your dad treats us like shit, tell us to get the out of his house. Were full breaded Sicilian but he accepts this half-breed as one of his own. I'm done with this Henry, why does he get's paid more than us?"

Sonny started to walk out the door until Henry stopped him with a gun pointed at him. "So that's what this is about, the money. He is my blood, he's a Cartone and that comes before anything. But you, your just a ungrateful prick who doesn't deserve a dime. And if you walk out that door I will shoot you in your back." Henry's tone was serious, he had it made up in his mind to kill Sonny. Nobody disrespected him or his family and lived with it not even a childhood friend. If Sonny would have stayed Henry would have took it as the liquor talking but by him walking out showed him that he truly didn't care about the family.

Sonny turned around to the gun in shock but maintained his composure. "Your gonna pull a gun on me Henry, after all these years. After all the things we've been through your gonna pull a gun on me! Well you might as well shoot." Sonny turned around and put his arms straight up leaving his back wide open, Henry just stood there with the gun on his friend.

Phil continued to count the money he didn't think Henry would shoot him it was two drunk friends taking an argument too far. Giovanni watched feeling bad because he egged it on. He could of stopped it but he was tired of Sonny's taunting and wanted to do something about it. He figured maybe a fight would break out but something like this is not what he expected.

"If you walk out that door Sonny I'm gonna shoot you, and that's a promise." Henry said with a mug on his face. His eyes were narrow and you can tell he was waiting to pull the trigger even though he didn't want to do it. Sonny turned his back on Henry and took a step towards the door.

"Don't do it Sonny, I swear to you I will kill you!" Henry threatened. He was crying at this point watching his friend take his final steps. Sonny kept walking towards the door once his foot hit the threshold Henry shot him four times in the back as tears fell down his face. His friend was dead.

Phil jumped out of his skin he didn't think there was anyway Henry would kill their friend of ten years. Phil turned in his chair and dropped a stack of money as he ran over to Sonny and checked his pulse and it was confirmed that he was dead. Giovanni just watched silently he didn't move until he looked at Henry sit with his eyes closed. He felt a little sorrow but not enough to feel any harsh feelings for his cousin. What Henry did was cold-blooded but that's the way it went down.

"You guys don't have to help me, I'm gonna take care of this myself." Henry said coldly as he got up, picked up Sonny's body and attempted to figure out what he was going to do about his fallen friend that he killed in cold blood. Giovanni went back to counting the money as Phil sat back down with his hands in his head. It finally hit him that with Henry he was in way too deep.

⸻

Carlo Delena the Mob boss of California sat in a limousine with his trusted bodyguard Carman and Charlie Cartone. Carlo was a man who been in the life longer then Paul Cartone and when Paul came to be a top earner is when tension began to rise between the two. Carlo didn't want to share his territory. Carlo was used to running the drug game for the mob not sharing the responsibility. Carlo was impatient and it was obvious in his demeanor. He controlled almost every neighborhood in California besides the black areas similar to the situation with the Cartones and Tony. Another thing was that Carlo was known by the feds and watched so he wasn't making nearly as much money as Cartone's were in the dope game. He also didn't supply the black parts of California either, like Tommy Cartone did with Larry.

He wasn't in his area which had him nervous also being in the black part of town unsettled him every time he was there. Carlo had reached a desperate moment because he was about to do something he never thought he would do in his life and that was work with a family member of an enemy and somebody who was black.

"So did you convince Tommy that it wasn't us responsible for Paul's death because that's very important to do if we want to wipe them out and take back my state. The other boss's won't contest us getting it if the Cartone family is out the way." Carlo spoke to everybody as if they didn't know anything. He figured being a boss gave him all the answers even though most of the time he spoke common knowledge.

"I tried the best I could, he's skeptical. I told him that Tony Taylor could had done it also but that's not our only problem." Charlie got nervous when he was speaking about Henry because he assured Carlo there wouldn't be any snags in his plan to hand Carlo the coke game so he can have a crime monopoly in California.

"If you're talking about the young Cartone I already know he's made some waves, they're already calling him the young Paul Cartone, but he's small fish still, Tommy's the old trout I'm worried about. Who knows, I might even be able to give the kid a job one day but I need you to take care of Tommy, it's vital. And what about this Tony character." Carlo asked.

"It's the same situation as Tommy. He's retired and handed over the reigns to his son who's another young kid out the making some moves. He's the on who's making trouble for Larry." Charlie could see that Carlo didn't care too much about the black dealers and his attention was on Tommy but once Carlo heard his big scheme he would be excited because the bottom line would be Tommy Cartone's demise.

"So this guy we're meeting, the one who has me over here in this god forsaken neighborhood, what's his story?" Carlo asked. Just the smell of the air, even though it was a nice area not the rough part of town bothered him. He sat on his high horse but the chance to take out Tommy was too good to pass up. A few years ago Tommy hit his son Joey and the other Boss's made him let it go but he still wanted revenge. When he hit Paul the boss's didn't do anything to punish Carlo. It was very important that the Tommy hit wouldn't come back on him because the powers that be made him stop at Paul. Any further action would cost him his life.

"He's Tony's bodyguard." Charlie stated.

"And that means what to me?" Carlo asked slightly irritated.

"He's going to be involved in my plan to get them to take each other out and keep our hands clean." Charlie said with a look of pride on his face seeing that Carlo liked the idea.

"That sounds good it keeps the heat off of my family so you want me to meet him and I will if he shows up, those moleys are never on time for anything. I don't want to be here longer than I have to, do you understand that?" Carlo said staring Charlie down.

"Yeah Carlo, he's on his way." Charlie was starting to get angry at Leroy for making him look bad in front of the mob boss. Maybe Leroy didn't have an idea about how important Carlo Delena was but he should of and if he wanted to have the whole area that Tony had to make the coke game his, he better recognize that this man was the one who could make it possible.

Just like clockwork Leroy knocked on the limo window and as it rolled down he saw Carman's face looking at him.

"I'm here to speak with Mr. Delena." Leroy said looking inside the limo very impressed with it. The door swung open and he sat down licking potato wedge grease off of his fingers. Carlo signaled for the driver to pull off and his driver obliged. The car went into motion carrying the occupants around the block and kept rolling.

"Sorry I'm late fellas' but I hope it gave you a chance to talk about what I can do for you and how you can help me." He was watching all the serious faces and when he noticed he was the only one smiling he stopped and just watched them.

"I was telling Mr. Delena how me and you are gonna set up Tommy and make it look like Tony did it so that way it will make it smoother for us to get you your territory that you asked for." Charlie was talking to Leroy like he had a learning disability, he didn't want Leroy to talk too much. God forbid that he said the wrong thing and got himself killed.

Leroy picked up on Charlie's assumptions about blacks and how they act. The way Leroy saw it they all were gangsters and he was going to speak the way he wanted but still keep it respectful. These crackers ain't going to change the way I talk, he thought. But he got the feeling that if he used slang or talked slick that they wouldn't understand him so he had to check his language in that manner which annoyed him.

"Yeah, I'm gonna convince Tony that it was Tommy that tried to hit Tony's son and I'm gonna hit Henry so Tommy believes it was Tony." Leroy said proudly. Charlie forgot how Carlo had just said that he might give Henry a job one day so his stomach dropped but when he realized that Carlo was thinking about it he didn't worry about Carlo not agreeing with the idea.

"That's not a bad idea, it's ironic also so I like it. That's like father and son versus father and son. When can you make it happen?" Carlo asked. Scanning Leroy he was impressed with him and he could tell it was more Leroy's idea than Charlie's.

Charlie was thinking ahead, about the aftermath he hoped this hit is what will make him a made man in the Delena family who had more clout than the Cartones. Carlo was the original boss out in California and to some of the mob Paul just came and took some of Carlo's territory which declined his authencity.

Charlie was one hundred percent Sicilian and he hated the fact that Paul wanted to be separate from a family and now that he was dead and the rest of his family would be dead he would no longer have to feel guilty about joining the Delena family which is what he wanted.

"So Leroy, for this favor in return you want the territory that you moleys are fighting over right?" Carlo asked. Leroy nodded his head dismissing the fact that this man called him a disrespectful name. He just wanted a chance to be the kingpin. "Okay, once it's done you got it, I'll loan you some keys and we'll come up with a nice business arrangement, I'm a very fair man so you'll have no problem." That was music to his ears and all he had to do was betray his friend for years. "And you Charlie for this favor you want to be a made man in my family right?" Carlo asked.

"Yeah Carlo!" Charlie responded excitedly, he was waiting for Carlo to say the word and give him his guarantee. Then once Tommy is dead you will be a made man apart of my family I guarantee it." Charlie wanted to kiss the man he felt so good and in an instant the limo pulled over.

"Call me when it's all taken care of." Carlo said coolly, and Carman opened the door for the two of them to get out. Standing on the curb Charlie looked at Leroy and nodded his head at him.

"Don't make me look bad, or it's gonna be bad for you do you understand me." Charlie snapped. His future rode on Leroy's ability to manipulate Tony and Leroy understood that as Charlie walked off Leroy grabbed his groin area and spat on the ground. He often wondered why Charlie talked like he was the one calling the shots when he was in fact in need of Leroy. He wasn't as cunning or war equipped. All those years with Tony made him ready, but a four man hit at this magnitude was going to take some time and careful strategy. If Charlie planned on Leroy rushing this he had another thing coming.

"Don't worry about me white boy!" He yelled. "I'll handle my business." He said to himself much lower like he had to convince himself that he could do it. He turned around and went back into Roscoe's chicken and waffles.

Tony had found out from a girl he used to mess with that Larry had been trying to get with her for years. She wasn't going to do anything with him but he convinced her that today would happened to be the day when she stopped giving him the run around and finally was going to give him some action.

"Make sure he doesn't touch me Tony." She said seriously.

"I promise he won't have sex with you." He responded. She still cringed at the thought of that man's hands on her. It made her body crawl in disgust.

For a long time she would tell him no matter how much money he had he couldn't pay her to sleep with him but after a lot of persistence he got her to at least lie to him and entertain the thought. He wasn't paying her for sex, but he been spending money on her to get her to this point for months, or so he thought. He'd been buying her clothes, shoes, fur coats, jewelry, and other things but she been having a thing for Tony since she was a teenager.

Tony was talking to her on the night Mac was shot and the conversation of Larry came up. A light bulb went off in his head. He knew Larry would so eager to finally feel this woman that his alarms would be down and it would be easy to get to him. So he convinced her to really seduce him and let Tony creep into the home unnoticed and he would give her fifty thousand dollars of Larry's money that she knew the location to. She could easily take money from Larry herself but she knew he would kill her. He told her to call him the next day and they would go into more details of the plan so it would go down to perfection.

The next day came and Tony talked to her. He told her he would be at Larry's house in an hour. She told him Larry constantly looks for cars so he decided to have Leroy drop him off. He told her to unlock the door and move the curtain three times to let him know it was unlocked. Once Tony was in the house he assured her that he could take care of the rest. Tony hung up the phone with her, hopped in his car and threw on his murder one gloves.

A hour passed and he got dropped off down the street from Larry's house by Leroy.

"Come back in about fifteen minutes alright." He told Leroy. Leroy nodded but in his mind he was thinking that Tony only had a couple more orders to give him before he was the one giving orders. He thought that he could catch Tony getting in the car after killing Larry and hit him then. The Element of surprise can catch any man but he knew Tony had a sixth sense when it came to war and he seen it first hand so he dismissed that idea. He just kept thinking about a plan to get him.

Tony got out of the car with his gun in the back of his pants. He waited across the street at a tree of a neighbor's house who wasn't home. He watched patiently in the shadows right behind the tree.

Larry lived in style he didn't have a huge house but the inside was decked out. He spent his money on the latest everything. Electronics, furniture everything you could imagine was the most expensive.

He didn't save any money and that was evident. There was no since of a home, it was party central. It was also sloppy because he gave his maid the whole day off.

Inside his room Larry was laying on his bed in his boxers being entertained by a seductive dance from the woman. She had on a bra and panties and surprisingly her behind looked better in panties then naked. Her breast were full and ran out of her bra. She was brown skinned and her hair was long and curly. She had the perfect face shape which showed off her cheekbones. Her face wasn't too thin and her cheekbones weren't too high. She had hazel eyes but her only flaw was her forehead was slightly large. Larry's nature had risen to it's height and he was getting to the point where he was ready to burst. But every time he would grab her she would shake her finger at him.

"Wait a minute, trust me, you've waited this long just give me a minute." She was trying to figure out a way to get him to take his eyes off of her so she can go unlock the door then the idea hit her.

"Give me a kiss daddy." She said seductively. As Larry tried to ram his tongue down her throat she stopped him and shook her head. "No, no, please go brush your teeth Larry that's nasty." Larry didn't get insulted as he ran to the bathroom in his room and the girl ran to the front door. She quickly unlocked the door, waved the curtain three times then ran back into the room and laid on the bed. Larry came out of his boxers with an full erection.

"No more four play baby, I need to feel that kitty cat, I've been waiting too long." Larry said with a raspy tone in his voice.

"It's ready for you baby." She responded laying her head back. Larry hopped on the bed and started roughly kissing her, in her mind she was praying for Tony to hurry up and rescue her from this animal.

Tony walked up to the door and cracked it open. He heard growls and the sounds of moaning that he could tell was fake. It was de javu` of San Francisco when he was about to kill Mario, the silence, the hunt and the prey would never know what was coming. He walked down the steps and as he took a step his heart started pounding. Larry had her legs open and was preparing for penetration while the girl was sweating and hoping that Tony would appear before Larry could enter her.

Tony kept stalking them and he raised his gun up as he turned the corner of the bedroom. He saw Larry just as he was about to enter the woman and whistled. Larry turned around and jumped out of his skin. His penis lost it's erection and he didn't even think to cover his naked body, he was scared straight. His eyes were watching Tony's gun and his hands were up in the air.

Tony kept the gun on him as he walked to the bed and sat down on it. He was staring Larry in the eye and the fear was actually making his blood boil. He thought Larry would at least act tough and hide his fear but that wasn't the case. He was supposed to be a worthy adversary but he turned out to be a coward. Even in the face of death Mario showed no fear, Tony couldn't respect a man like Larry.

"Tony, what do you want man, do you want me to quit the game and leave it for your son, I'll do it!" Larry was erratic. His arms started trembling and he dropped to his knees naked and embarrassed. "Do you want that bitch, take her I don't care, don't kill me man."

The scene was playing out exactly like on Scarface where Tony Montana killed Frank and he was begging for his life trying to offer him money and his woman Tony thought. It was funny to him hearing Larry call his name while on his knees but at least Frank wasn't naked.

Tony had enough of Larry, he was going to leave him lying there naked so when the police do find him he'll be embarrassed in the after life.

"You tried to kill my boy Larry. Why didn't you ever put a hit on me? You were too scared!" Tony exclaimed trying to keep calm the sight of him started to sicken him and it was time to murder the coward. Tony shot him in the head twice and his body dropped to the awkwardly. He walked over him and seen a box of Kleenex. He tossed it to the woman and she looked up at him confused.

"Grab your money and then wipe down everything you touched. You did good baby if he got more then fifty thousand take all of it." She smiled at him as he turned to walk out the door.

"Tony!" She called. He turned around and looked at her. "What about your cut of the money, are you sure you don't want it?" She wasn't a money hungry woman she just used Larry, but when it came to Tony she would give him the world if he asked her too.

"Nah baby you earned that don't forget to wipe everything you touched because that's important." She nodded her head swiftly and got to work as Tony walked through the house and out the front door. Leroy was sitting out there waiting for him and Tony walked up to the passenger side and got in.

"Did it go alright?" Leroy asked. Tony smiled at him and that told him everything he needed to know, Larry was gone and out the way so in Leroy's mind Tony and Terell where the two people standing between him and dominance. "Where's the girl at?" Leroy asked.

"She's in there cleaning the place up." Tony said as Leroy pulled off, he stopped the car quickly.

"Your gonna leave her to do it?" Leroy asked shocked. Tony just looked at him and he knew Tony wanted him to shut up and drive. Leroy started to smile in his head because it was evident that Tony was slipping, he would of never did that before and the fact that he did let him know that with a little more time he would be vulnerable enough to get killed.

Mac is at the spot watching the action on the streets. He always felt it necessary to keep his ears to the streets even though he was involved in big deals. He learned that from Terell which was something that kept him with a killer instinct. He was watching the movements of the nickel and dimmers. How they warned each other when the cops rolled by as well as the call for the cokeheads and heroin addicts. Needles sickened him just like it did everybody he was associated with that's why they left it for the more viscous dealers who could deal with those nasty kind of junkies. Crack wasn't the biggest thing it was just starting up but cocaine and heroin was in effect majorly.

Mac seen a young dealer name Kevin. His mom was a junkie and he used to rob dealers just to get her a fix. Mac took him under his wing and would always give him money and smoke weed with him because he noticed the young man's potential and figured he could breed game into him in order to use him one day if he needed. A man like Mac could never genuinely love somebody because he's so spiteful inside but he thought in his mind that he had love for some people and Kevin was one of them.

Kevin was little for his age but deadly. He carried around a knife and had used it a few times in his young years. He stabbed a couple of addicts who tried to rape his mother. He used it on a couple of kids that messed with him verbally and physically which was the situation that lead Mac to find him. He was beaten up badly by some older kids but one of them felt the wrath of the knife before he caught his massacre.

"What's up Mac, when you gonna put me on man? I need to get paid." Kevin asked as his puppy dog eyes stared right through Mac like he was looking at his soul. Mac shook his head. He could be messed up and have the little man doing something but he couldn't allow himself to do it. "I'm tired of taking handouts from you, I wonna earn the money you giving me and moms man." Kevin wiped his nose then looked down at his shoes. Mac felt bad, he would give him some dollars but the little man wanted to hustle and he couldn't put him on yet. Mac was waiting till he was at least thirteen but Kevin was only eight. Youngsters were hustling younger than that but Mac wasn't letting the streets grab this one yet. But the problem with that is if Mac didn't put him on somebody else would.

"Take this dough, it's more than I normally give you and if you want to earn your money stop robbing out here so I can keep you around Kevin because if you get hurt or locked I might flip out man, you supposed to hold me down right." Mac put both hands on his shoulders.

"Right!" Kevin responded.

"Then hold me down man, now go get your mom her fix, something to eat and some shoes or something.

Kevin ran off and Mac seen Rick coming out the spot placing his gun in the back of his pants. He noticed how Ricky and Terell where getting closer and started to dislike it. Ricky was just more trustworthy than him and he was just as hard so Mac figured eventually Ricky would be second and that meant getting more paper than him and Mac couldn't have that.

"We got a deal to make with the Asians man, Terell handling some business with Tony, you know where we going to meet them right?" Ricky asked. Mac responded how he usually did when somebody irritated him "Yeah, so he got you making phone calls for business, go get the car man."

Ricky looked at Mac for a second then shook his head, he seen what Mac's problem was and he knew it would happen but he really didn't care. Mac had done his job and introduced him to the man. Ricky walked down the street to where the car was parked and Mac's eyes bulged out of his head when he saw Phil, wearing a black leather coat, walking towards him.

At first he was shock to see Phil by himself after a violent fight in the neighborhood that broke out which was one of the last few racial tension fueled fights. It was the eighties but brutal racism still existed. Then he realized who he was and understood why because he was probably packing something that could blow holes the size of quarters in cats if they ran up on him.

"Look who's in the hood." Mac said as he seen Ricky pull up and honk the horn for him. "What you doing over here white boy?" Mac questioned.

"Let's talk in your um, establishment here for a second okay." Phil said with a smile on his face. He could see Mac's solemn face "Come on Mac it's nothing like that I think we can help each other.

Just a minute of your time, I see you got business to tend to well so do I." Mac turned around and Phil followed him into the store Ricky sat in the car and honked the horn obviously upset because Mac was making them late.

Mac was trying to figure out why Phil was there talking to him but he wasn't prepared for the reason. He was thinking that it could have been a set-up but he talked to him because it could be beneficial. There was something about Phil's mannerism that made him think that he had a proposition which was the case at hand.

Phil was shook when Henry killed Sonny. He didn't like murder at all but when it was somebody he cared about he hated it and wanted no parts of it. Money is what he loved and violence doesn't bring money so he decided to go and try to set up a truce. But he knew in order for him to keep getting money and to avoid a war, somebody had to go. He thought he'd talk to Mac and see where his head was at and how loyal he was to Terell.

"I've been hearing things about your man Terell. They're saying he's bout to get a hit put on him by some real mobsters and his pops. So when he's gone what are you going to do?" Phil questioned anticipating that his answer would have something to do with his personal gain and not the safety of Terell.

"That means there's an open spot in this game then. If Terell goes out he goes out, but don't get it confused man, I'm not coming to work for you or Henry." Mac said, missing the reason Phil asked the question being self-absorbed he assumed that Phil was on a recruiting mission.

"I know you won't, everybody wants to be a boss." Phil said.

"Why are you here man? I ain't got time for all this small talk." Mac said impatiently.

"The mob boss of California won't get any money over here himself but he'll supply this area, so take out the competition and you'll be the man with the connect. Do you understand that my friend?" Phil asked. Mac looked at him unimpressed.

"How do you know this?" Mac asked.

"Come on man, you don't have to ask that. Think about it and I'll be back in a couple of days for your answer, okay Mac. All we gotta do is hit them both and we'll be good." Phil walked out of the spot and through the grocery store when he exited out of the front he saw an angry Ricky sitting in the car. He smiled at him and walked down the street. Mac came out next staring Phil down as he walked away. It was obvious he was thinking about the deal he was just offered.

"Who was that?" Ricky asked wondering who has holding them up to get the money.

"Just some honkey, he was trying to get on with some weight, I was hooking up a deal so come on and let's go get this money man."

Tony sat at his bar with Brian and Terell having drinks. Terell was smoking a joint and they were talking about Brian's relationship with Elana. Neither one of them had objections about it.

"You still going to have to wait on her man, my niece ain't like these other little girls around here. Are you sure your going to be faithful when you have them cold shower nights?" Tony asked testing to see if Brian was right for his niece because even though he loved Brian like a son he wouldn't let anybody hurt Elana. "Because if you hurt her, I'm gonna have to beat you up boy!" Tony warned.

Brian wanted to change the subject so he brought up the first thing that came to mind which was Leroy coincidently. He hadn't seen him around lately and when he did he was always acting distant. Brian noticed it and figured he'd bring it up to Tony to get the conversation off the topic of his relationship between him and Elana.

"What's been up with Leroy, I haven't seen him around lately?" Brian asked like the question was unintentionally asked.

"I don't know." Tony responded "He has been acting funny lately." Tony for the first time really pondered on the sly comments and lack of conversation coming from Leroy, the little things all started to add up. Tony didn't want to believe it and forced it to the back of his mind he would need something blatant. Leroy could be stressed out about some personal things going on in his life. Him and Tony never really discussed things like Leroy's relationships or his family. Tony had recognized that he was been catching himself becoming more paranoid recently which is how this game could turn you if you let it.

"What's wrong pop?" Terell asked seemingly concern about what his father was thinking, just like Tony seen Leroy acting weird lately Terell noticed that his father was acting the same way. Since Mac got shot they fell off the same page on how to run the business. Terell had been at it for months now which was not even a sixteenth of the amount of time that Tony but into this game but his time was over.

"When are we going to deal with Cartone pop, you got Larry out the way now when are we gonna hit them." Terell was getting irritated with his father's lack of urgency but Tony was waiting to see if he could use Gina as a way to see where Tommy's head was at.

Gina and Tony weren't best of friends but they still talked from time to time. Gina had never moved on after Jimmy and Tony was a constant player so even though there was no sexual companionship, they're was definitely a friendship. He knew that she wouldn't do to Tommy what she did to Mario but she would let him know if she got the vibe that Tommy was going to try something even if she didn't want to believe it.

"I told you I'm waiting on Gina to let me know what's up with that. Hold on man, just chill." Tony put his hope in Terell's ability to calm down at the right time which wasn't smart because of his son's temper and problems with patience were getting worse and he could see it. But Terell was still listening to him which was a good thing.

"Henry's not going to make a move against you yet because he's too busy waiting on you to retaliate for the dope he robbed you for. He's still trying to get from under his father's name. Believe me, you're not that much different" Tony poured a shot and drunk it then poured another one. Terell thought about what his father said and it did make since to him.

"I'm gonna get him soon pop, and there's going to be a time when you can't talk me out of it." Just as Terell finished his comment Leroy came into the bar and sat down. He snatched the drink from in front of Tony and drunk it then poured another one and set it in front of him. He did like it was a big joke that's why he poured Tony one so fast. He walked around the bar to where Terell was standing and sat down. He pulled out a quarter and started flipping it.

"Why are you flipping that coin?" Terell asked. Tony was staring at Leroy and at this point he could see the change in his attitude but again it was another small change but it really bothered him. Leroy had no reason to be cocky unless some big things was going to happen in his favor, and since Terell wasn't going no where it hit Tony that Leroy might be planning something against him.

"No reason youngsta, I got the car ready boss." Leroy said like he was Morgan Freeman on Driving Mrs. Daisy, Brian even looked shocked at his comment. Terell didn't really notice but Brian and Tony could see the change in attitude like he had a problem with Tony. Leroy walked out of the bar area as Tony watched him.

"He's up to something and I'm gonna find out what it is." Tony said calmly but Terell was tired of hearing about waiting.

"Stop the bullshit man! If you think somebody trying to kill you, you kill them first. You know the rules to this. I'd shoot all of them at once, Larry, Tommy, Henry, Leroy, hell even Carlo Delena, POP! I know you want to strategize, but waiting ain't the best strategy all the time." Brian was mad that he even brought it up all because he wanted to get the attention off him Elana he damned near started another world war between his father and brother. He figured he could lighten the mood by bringing it back up.

"You two are ruining my moment, I'm a man in love and I wanted to share my happiness?" Brian said, Tony and Terell both laughed at him and Tony poured shots for the three of them

"Look at him Terell, a man in love, she got him acting like a sucka." Tony said as they took the shots slammed the glasses down on the bar top. Tony looked at his son's and couldn't be more proud of both of them at that moment. They were very different but both of them very good at their lifestyles and that's all he could really ask for. Brian more than Terell though. He was starting to see that his son may not make it and turn into another hustler's tragedy, but he wasn't worried about Brian at all.

Terell laughed and joked with his father but the feeling of anger didn't go anywhere. He was starting to loose faith in the man and he needed him to be dependable, he needed to count on him.

Tony walked out of the bar to take a ride with Leroy as Ricky walked in. Ricky sat down and greeted Brian and Terell with handshakes. "Mac was talking to some white boy today, he said it was a potential buyer but it was something funny about it man, you might wonna check it out. I know we got problems with them Italians, I've never seen him but the white boy he was talking to was Italian." Ricky said which caught Terell off guard. Here was some new cat he put on, showed his savageness a couple of times and now he was suggesting that Mac is doing something sneaky which he has never done before. Terell was confused about this situation.

He watched Ricky as he sat down and took a shot his mind was assessing the situation at the speed of light. It was only two options Ricky was trying to turn them against each other and get rid of Mac, or Mac was trying to plot against him and Ricky was just maintaining his realness, which Terell saw in him from the beginning. So it was your classic time versus character factor. Do you trust the person you've known longer or the person with the better character.

"I'll look into it." Is all Terell said as he poured himself another shot and slammed it.

Brian was outside of Elana's front door and her back was against the door. The imagery created from the two suggest he's on the outside of her emotional wall. He's thought that she might be getting cold feet about them or maybe her family is trying to come between them. It had been a few months since the carnival and the last couple of weeks she was distant, not too distant but she definitely wasn't acting like she was at first. If he was a betting man he would bet that her family were coming in between them which was the case.

Something that her mom said stuck in her mind and it was because Gina knew about experiences with love when it collides with your family. She saw the similar signs her mother saw. Jimmy and Brian were a like, they both were good people morally at the same time they both were non-judgmental. But she couldn't turn her feelings all the way off so she gave him light kisses, sometimes she didn't answer his phone calls and every time he would say things to make her heart melt she would smile when she really wanted to spill her heart and tell him how she felt.

Brian wasn't giving up but he didn't want to bring up this new act she had going on. To him if it was meant to be he would break the wall down that she had up, if not then it was on to the next girl. It wasn't true thoughts of a romantic but he wasn't Romeo. He was almost in love with her but she wasn't the key to his world. Not even his father and brother were the key to his world. The only thing that could get that title was his babies if he would ever have any.

It was killing Elana to have to put on this act. Sometimes she wished Brian would just leave her alone so she wouldn't have to do it but on the other hand that fact that he stayed around turned her on completely. he was showing mental toughness she hadn't seen from nobody of the opposite sex.

Brian had her backed up on the door and was moving in for a kiss when she stopped him, pulled him towards her and gave him a half passionate but sweet innocent kiss on the lips. She turned around to walk in the house when Brian put his arm around her waist. Just that touch made her stomach go into jolts of excitement.

"My mom is in here Brian, we got to pick this up another time." She said trying avoid any conversation or want he might have of coming into her house.

"Pick what up, there's hasn't been a lot, if you lost interest then that's cool, just tell me." Brian said trying go get an understanding of the sudden change of intimacy that she was showing him and it wasn't just the affection, it was the amount of time they spent together as well as the lack of conversation between the two. She didn't open up to him about her positive thoughts, everything was about the cold harsh world they lived in and the violence around them. She always brought up how bad her Uncle was and how he could turn Brian into something that he wasn't. Brian was unaware of where all this was coming from and he wanted answers.

"I told you I might not be ready for that step." She said hoping he was just talking about a physical thing but she knew better than that and she had to prepare for an excuse of why she'd been so distant lately furthermore Brian knew her so he could tell when she was lying.

"You know that's not what I'm talking about!" Brian was getting irritated but he didn't want to pressure her. "Look, I'm not tripping on you and how you feel so give me a call whenever you really trying to open up." Brian turned around and walked off, as he was walking down the street Elana got mad herself but she was mad at her mother more for putting those doubts about their relationship in her head and making her second guess the fact that they could be together. She felt like she was going to loose the best thing that ever happened to her and she didn't know if she could allow that to happen.

Elana walked into the house and ignored her mother as her mothered watched television. Gina could see that her daughter was mad at her so she decided to do something she should of done a long time ago, tell her the whole story of what happened ten years ago, so she could really understand why her and Brian couldn't be together and giver her some perspective of why she should move on with her life and get over him.

"Elana why don't you come here." Gina asked politely.

"I already followed you're order to cut things off with Brian. I still see him but I feed him with a long handled spoon because of you. What else do you want from me." Elana responded with tons of attitude in her voice.

"Please come sit and talk to me." Gina repeated. When she did receive an answer she figured her daughter wasn't going to talk to her so she just blurted the first truth out. "Your father wasn't killed by some robber." It took a couple of seconds but Elana was standing in front of her mother with her hand placed on her hips. The look on her face was angry because she had a feeling there were a lot more lies to come. "Sit down." Gina said patting the seat next to her like it was a soft puppy which is how she treated her daughter's emotions over the past years. She felt that Elana was too fragile to experience the cold world but she felt that time had to stop. Elana sat next to her mother anticipating to hear the real reason why her father was no longer living.

"You know your Uncle Tony and my family had been fighting over this stupid drug game for years and one night your Uncle Tony killed your Uncle Vinny. The words stung her heart but she was in too much shock and anticipation to cut her mom off. "So in retaliation it was your uncle Mario who came and killed your father." Gina's heart started pounding and she almost instantly burst into tears. Every second that ticked was like a sharp knife ripping at the pit of her stomach and her flesh was being gouged metaphorically. Gina gave her a moment to absorb the information before saying the most hardest part of the story for her.

"So Uncle Tony started this because of this drug business?" Elana asked roughly. She was trying to understand it but she couldn't wrap her mind around it. She thought it had to be something else that made Tony kill her uncle Vinny and start this chain reaction of death.

"Well, it was that amongst other things. Even without the drugs involved my family and your father's family never got along. Mario was always threatening Jimmy, taunting him and your father had nothing to do with Vinny dying that was all Tony's doing." Gina said still trying to avoid her part in this story.

"So what part of this are you leaving out mom?" She inquired as she watched the tears start to flow from her mother's face.

"I was so mad at Mario that I went to Tony and I told him exactly where Mario would be at to have Tony kill him on his anniversary." She broke down at this point letting out soft sobs and burying her head in her hands. Elana couldn't believe her ears. She just sat there and watched her mother cry thinking about what she just heard.

She never was aware of all the corrupt and violent people she was related to and now that it had been exposed some part of her didn't feel sorry for all these deaths to these people except for her father. Her ideas of decency and good morals that were instilled in her came from people who had been killing and lying to each other, it sickened her. She didn't want to turn into a woman like her mother but she also thought about if it would be a possibility to murder for the man she loved if it was deep enough.

She thought about how Brian felt on the other side of the equation. She wondered if he could be caught up in all this treachery in the name of family honor and revenge. Her world had been tipped and as her mother cried her eyes out she figured that she wasn't going to allow her love for Brian to be affected by the past and she wouldn't hold back her feelings for him anymore because life isn't perfect and if you be too cautious in fear of past mistakes you won't get the full enjoyment out of it.

"Mom, Brian isn't daddy, and I'm not you. I can't speak for anybody else but I'm sure of that. I can't stay away from him because I love him and if I keep acting this way towards him I'm going to loose him. I don't care if we have to run away together." Gina looked at her daughter with pain still in her eyes, she knew Elana was making the wrong choice and she feared for what could happen to Brian.

"If you love him so much, you have to let him go Elana." Gina was all out of energy trying to reach her daughter, she knew Elana was becoming a woman and developing her own mind. If Gina's own father couldn't control her, what gave her the right to try and control her kids, she thought. Gina stood up and walked into the back room. Elana watched her mother and for the first time in Elana's life her mother looked worn and torn. She appeared to be mentally and emotionally drained. Gina's heart was lighter now that she got that secret off her chest to her daughter who was the only one that was left out of the loop.

Giovanni was told about it by his grandfather when he was fifteen and the way he seen it, father or not it's called eye for an eye, if you take one of mine I take one of yours. That philosophy is something that was incorporated in the survival of the fittest mind set.

Elana thought about this war brooding and maybe this time it could be stopped, but in order for it to happen she needed all the information. She was aware how mad Brian would be and how Mac might demand something in return that she would never give him which made her stop that thought of talking to Mac like a train, then she thought about a much better person her brother Giovanni.

Gina walked out of her house on her way to see her brother, she saw Tony's car parked outside of her house. She sighed as she walked to the window and leaned over it to get closer so people walking the streets wouldn't over hear they're conversation. She showed Tony a slight smile because even though she was still worried about Elana and Brian she was happy to see Tony but he would never know that.

Tony seen that Gina was looking better than she had in a long time so he assumed something big had changed and he was curious about it. "You look different, you got an extra spring in your step this mourning, what happened, did you find a man?" Tony asked with a sly smirk. Gina almost blushed it was just like Tony to say something like that she thought. She didn't need a man to make her feel better telling her daughter the truth after eight years of lying to her cleared her cautions.

"No Tony, I finally told Elana about what happened in San Francisco as well as the rest of our history." She was curious to see if Tony would get mad but he didn't. She looked over at Leroy and seen a look in his eyes that made her fell uneasy. It was like he was looking at her like a piece of meat so she felt like she was ready to leave. Leroy was intrigued in the fact that Tony wanted to see her especially with his plan to kill him and with her being Cartone's sister she might be the way to get them both he thought as he watched her like a hawk.

"Leroy why don't you go for a walk and let me and Gina talk alone for a minute." Tony ordered. He had some things to discuss with her concerning Tommy and he didn't trust Leroy. Gina felt relieved as she saw Leroy exit out of the driver's seat and walk down the street. She was on the way to see her brother but she felt like she could put that off for a few minutes to hear what Tony had to say. When she got in the seat and comfortable Tony started with the conversation.

"I need a favor form you? Leroy has turned on me and I think somebody in your family is trying to take my son out?" Tony said. Gina instantly declined. "No Tony, I don't want to get involved, my daughter is already wrapped up in this because of your son Brian, okay, so leave me out of it!"

Tony expected her to act like that so he took off his shades and stared at her. He used his eyes as a tool to get her to bring that wall she had up down. "Listen Gina, I don't want you to get involved in nothing but keeping your ears open. Spend more time around your house, listen out for me, give me a heads up, that's it. I can't keep Terell calm for much longer he's talking about hitting your whole family. He's like me all those years ago." Tony stated.

"Oh God!" Gina said. She remembered how Tony was. She was breaking down the more he spoke to her. "All you want is for me to let you know what my brother's plans are, if he has any." She asked making sure she understood what he was asking of her.

"Yes, that's it." Tony assured her. He definitely meant it, he seen how her setting Mario up messed with her head. He would never directly involve her in anything against her family again.

"I will call you if I hear something." She said as she was getting out of the car Tony slid over to the driver seat and drove off trying to find Leroy so they could handle business he honked the horn as he passed Gina who was entering the key in her car door so she could start it and get on the road to see her brother.

Before she drove off she looked across the street and seen Leroy again staring at her with that same devilish look. There was something about him that didn't sit well with her and it made her mind go to alert mode. She was going to mention it to Tony next time she talked to him.

Gina made her way down the street and thirty minutes later she arrived at the Cartone mansion. She didn't go there often and the last time she was there was when her father died and she spent a few days with her brother and son. Giovanni lived there and had been since he was sixteen, she loved her son but he spent so much time there when he became a teenager that he eventually just lived there. She drove through the gates and up to the front of the house. She stepped out and walked passed the guards and in front her father's study which was the first room past the front doors. She remember what Tony said and stood to the side of the open door as she could hear Charlie and Tommy talking.

"How do you know Tony is planning on hitting Henry, did you talk to the person planning on doing it. I don't know Charlie the more I talk to you the less I trust you." Tommy had been hearing things from Charlie about how he should not be so focused on the Delena family while Tommy was planning to hit them. Charlie was going against it, and every time Tommy would get close it's like Carlo would get tipped off.

"When I was gonna clip him at the restaurant he goes out the back door. How did he know about that Charlie, how did he know which door to go out of?" Tommy asked. He demanded answers he didn't want to kill his uncle but he would if he found out that he was working with the Delena family.

"How dare you ask me that? I loved your father, he was my baby brother and you accuse me of siding with the enemy, I could of stayed in Miami. You're getting side tracked away from this Tony issue, because he's the one that killed Paul." As soon as Gina heard her Uncle bring Tony into the conversation that's when she got suspicious and entered the room.

"Gina, what are you doing here?" Tommy asked as she approached him and kissed him on his cheek, then she approached her Uncle and did the same thing before sitting down in the office.

"I just came to see my brother, what were you guys talking about?" Gina inquired hoping to get some kind of information out of one of them because now her interest was obliged in their discussion.

"Just business, Charlie was just leaving though, right uncle." Tommy hinted to him that they would have to resume what they were talking about at a later time but his suspicions were definitely up about his uncle's connection with the Delena family and he felt he couldn't trust him which saddened his heart but he knew about the life he lived and how your own family could betray you.

"Yeah Tommy, sure thing we'll talk later, bye Gina." He said monotone as he walked out of the room, Gina stared at her brother. He felt her gaze and knew she wasn't buying what he told her, he knew she heard something he said and Tommy was wondering why was she so interested. She had made it a point to stay out of his affairs but suddenly she was milking him for information.

"You think Tony had something to do with killing papa don't you?" The question surprised him, he knew that she had gotten somewhat close to Tony years ago but he thought their friendship was over.

"What if I did, do you think otherwise, or do you already know something?" Tommy was now the one doing the questioning, his sister could be the missing piece in the puzzle he was trying to put together. She obviously didn't think he did it but he couldn't understand what made her so sure that he didn't do it. The fact that she was dead set on her theory concreted his suspicions about the Delena family.

"What I do know is that this war between you two died with Jimmy and Mario, why after all these years would it get re-started up again. It already went to the next generation, even though you and Tony have both let this business go you should be worried more about Henry." She stated.

Tommy felt that Henry's fate was in his hands and why he couldn't feel the same way about his father confused him but what he did know is this thing between the Cartone's and the Delena family had to end. At that moment he was sure that it was going to end soon because he was going to do something about it. If he happened to be wrong about Tony again then he would have to deal with that later. Then he took it one step further, he might need Tony's help with his plan.

"If he didn't do it Gina, you have him meet with me sometime soon and we can settle this whole thing. I might need his help with doing what I have planned." Tommy said, Gina didn't ask questions just knowing that her brother believed her and supported her defending Tony was enough.

It had been a while since Giovanni and Elana had a brother and sister heart to heart talk and there they were in their deceased Grandfather's yard. The courtyard made them go back to when they were kids playing in it with Henry. Times had changed from then and it was a shame to see how many lives had been taken and bonds had been broken all because of race and money. It was no question that their love for each other ran deep as the sea but with their total completely different outlooks and views on life, it was hard for them to be close. Giovanni was aware of the relationship blooming between Brian and his sister and thought it was a bad idea just because of the war between the families.

He had nothing against Brian, in fact when they were younger they got along very well but when you're on two opposite sides of the battle field friendships don't matter. His main concern was his sister not getting caught in the cross fire because she loved him. He knew what Elana wanted to talk to him about but he wondered how she was going to approach him. If she thought she could get him to turn on Henry she had another thing coming so he was anticipating to hear his sister out.

"I know all about what really happened to our father and what mom and Uncle Tony did to Uncle Mario. I expected everybody else to keep it from me but not you Vanni." Giovanni was thrown off guard a little bit, he was always told to forget about it, he wouldn't of even known if his grandfather didn't get drunk one night and decide to test his loyalty to their side of the family. He thought if Giovanni could understand why his father had to die then he was a Cartone and when Giovanni didn't show any anger and kept it to himself Paul knew that Giovanni's loyalty was with the Cartone family.

"That was a long time ago Elana. Is that all you came to talk to me about?" Giovanni said impatiently. Elana stared at her brother his coldness and distance hurt her feelings he was once a vibrant young man but she felt that every since Jimmy died and he started spending more time with her grandfather and Henry that the life got sucked out of him. She watched her brother's mannerisms and they were solid like a soldier. What she failed to realize was that nobody created Giovanni, this is how he was and he did look at her as a traitor and wished they could have been closer.

"Now Henry and Terell are starting this war back up over drugs and you and Brian are caught in it." Elana expressed while she grabbed her brother's hands and searched for some compassion in his eyes. Giovanni turned away from Elana, he did feel nervous about the events that was coming to head. Henry was making a lot of noise in the coke game and he thought he was starting to go too hard to fast. Giovanni saw Scarface like everybody else and that movie was like a blueprint on how to come and die fast in the game.

"Don't make this about me, you're worried about your boyfriend." Giovanni said coldly. It almost made him smile on the inside to say it. It amused and pleased him that she finally had some interest in the opposite sex he thought she turn out to be gay or something.

Elana was hurt by his remarks and drew back from Giovanni a little bit. Realizing he hurt his sister he instantly felt bad he could see the tears in her eyes starting to come.

"Yes he is my boyfriend and this whole situation is driving a wedge between us and yes Henry and Terell are my first cousins, but you're my brother and I love you. Henry and Terell can do whatever they want but I don't want you or Brian to get caught in they're problems. This life is not what Brian's going to live, and this isn't what you want to do with yours." Elana stated.

"What else do I got?" Giovanni asked. Elana was waiting to crush his rebuttal.

"You can manage any entertainment establishment, I remember you used to torture me when we were kids pretending to host all those guys from the cat pack." She responded.

"You mean the rat pack." He stated smiling. "Sammy Davis was my favorite, don't tell Henry I said that though." Giovanni felt a little better by talking with his sister and it gave him a little insight to make some type of attempt to convince Henry to slow down. He knew he wouldn't turn his back on his cousin but if anybody could get Henry to at least calm down on his boldness it would be Giovanni.

"All I want you to do is at least talk to Brian for me, and if you two can't come to a conclusion then I wash my hands with the situation. I just can't sit back and not at least try something." She locked her green eyes in on her brother and could tell he was thinking about it.

"Alright, tell him to meet me at mom's house tomorrow and we can talk. This ain't no set-up is it?" Giovanni joked but the thought part way crossed his mind she was her mother's daughter.

"Shut up!" She smacked his arm playfully as they both stood to their feet and started to walk towards the front gates. Elana looked around the yard and scoped a beautiful landscape that she remember playing in a little bit as a child. When they reached the front gates they saw they're mother driving down it and gave each other a strange look.

Gina stopped a second just as surprised to see Elana as she was to see her. "I see you came to talk to your brother like I came to talk to mine. Do you want a ride home?" She asked hoping that her daughter had forgiven her some for her dishonesty.

Elana didn't respond as she hugged her brother and walked around to the passenger side of the car.

"Are you still coming by tomorrow?" Gina asked Giovanni as he walked to the window and reached in and gave his mother a hug.

"Yeah." He said and she drove off and out the gates, he turned and walked back into the Cartone mansion still unsure about the decision that he just made to talk to Brian.

Elana sat on the steps of Tony's porch in deep thought about Brian. It had been three days since they talked and she was worried he had washed his hands with her. He wasn't returning her phone calls or coming by and she needed to speak with him to get him to understand why she was being so distant and that she was in love with him. Furthermore she felt that if he talked to her brother it could make this situation between Terell and Henry go away even though that was highly unlikely.

Luckily Giovanni was willing to talk to him. She hoped he could understand where Brian was coming from since he was open to the talk. Giovanni wasn't used to giving his sister advice on relationships so he told her to just give him some space but don't wait forever on anybody, let alone a man. She wanted him so bad that her mind, body and heart ached for him. His face invaded her dreams and she would wake up wishing his hands were there to comfort and hold her. She could feel strong sexual desires creeping in her mind and it was driving her crazy.

One night she was tempted to explore her body herself but only got as far as caressing her thighs then she stopped and cried. It had been a hard three days for her and she wondered what Brian was doing. She wondered if he thought about her or not. She wondered if he was between another girls sheets which would break her heart into a million pieces. The bottom line she came up with in her mind was that he was giving her a taste of her own medicine, just in a more brutal form. He was completely cutting her off.

Elana looked up and met Brian's face. His face was cold but his eyes had the same warmth and compassion as she was used to. She stood up and hugged him but he kept his arms to his side, as she let him go she kept looking at him.

"What's up?" He asked coolly as he walked passed her. "Do you want to go inside?" He was trying to play cool and she could tell. He was just as happy to see her as she was to see him and the love in her was shooting fireworks. Her little breakdown and wall building practices were forgiven and all it took was a few days of dealing with him ignoring her.

"Yes. I have something important to tell you about the way I've been acting lately." She said as he was unlocking the door and opened it. She walked passed him and through the ajar door as he looked her up and down he got that familiar, nature rising effect that she had on him. He followed her into the bar area and they sat down on opposite sides of the bar.

"I'm happy we got what we have Brian and the reason why I was so distant to you was because of the fact my mother didn't think it was a good idea we see each other and just for a minute I believed her. But I couldn't just not see you so instead I kept a wall up so we wouldn't get any closer." She knew her explanation wasn't a good one but it was the truth. Brian just looked at her. He was amazed how she could feel so bad about the way she felt. To him, he was the immature one, at least she didn't completely shut down, he felt like his actions were worse. He ignored her and basically forced her to come back and initiate some kind of re-kindlement of what they had which never had an official title. He was on his way to call her when he got home to make an attempt for her to reach out to him.

"I'm sorry for acting the way I did, I should of realized what you were going through and gave you space." He said. Just like that all was forgiving and the two found themselves on one of the couches kissing passionately and this time there was no holding back. Elana had her hands unbuckling Brian's belt and as he felt it his manhood reached full attention. She stroked it up and down, with slight tugs at the base. His body relaxed.

They were kissing passionately as he grabbed at her well rounded but firm thighs. He rubbed his other hand up her stomach to the bottom of her succulent breast. She moaned as he caressed around her nipple while he softly pinched it. The two bodies were both in pure bliss as the foreplay continued and was at full speed.

Elana straddled Brian out of pure instinct and started to grind his middle region while he planted his hands on her ass, she stopped as she realized she could barely contain herself and a couple of more seconds she would be naked on her uncle's couch losing her virginity.

"Wait Brian!" she said halfway out of breath. I want this but not like this, not right now, but soon." She said putting major emphasis on the word soon.

"How soon, you mean like this weekend. I can get us a nice hotel room and make is special." Brian said still ready to burst in his pants.

"That sounds good, but I need to know if you been with anybody else for these past three days." Elana questioned, she knew his answer wouldn't change anything but she wanted to look into his eyes and see if he would lie to her.

"No." Brian said honestly. I've been trying to figure what's been wrong with you, I told you how I feel about sex. I'm not a virgin but I don't just put my stuff in anything, especially when my heart isn't in it and my heart is wrapped up in you, all the way like never before.

"Are you trying to tell me something?" Elana wanted so bad to hear him say that he loved her, she felt that he did but she wanted to hear it just as bad as she wanted to say it. She got from off of his lap and fixed her dress properly and stared at Brian mesmerizing him with those green eyes.

"Since I've been back and we been spending all this time together I would have been in love with you years ago. But now I see you and it's a reality and no longer a dream I've never been so sure about anything in my life that I love you and want to see where it's going to take us. I love you Elana Taylor." His words were so sincere it struck her heart and it was the most beautiful thing she ever heard in her life. Brian was like a dream for her, the kind of gem that was in the neighborhood filled with criminals and gangsters, or whimps that she felt couldn't protect her. Brian had that balance that every girl wanted and was glad to have him.

"I love you too Brian Robinson." Elana said.

Now she was worried about asking him to talk to her brother which could start a fight after all that leeway she just made but it was something that she had to do. So instead of coming out with it she decided to talk about something else to ease her into that conversation.

"Another thing I've been dealing with is being lied to by my mother about my father's death. Apparently he didn't get robbed and shot by some mugger." She started. Brian felt his stomach turn in knots as she talked. He remember clearly the night of the carnival when she asked him not to lie to her and when she was talking about her dad's death he knew the whole story. "My uncle Mario killed him and uncle Tony and my mom killed him and so on and so on, which I've been dealing with." The thought of all that betrayal just made her head hurt and Brian noticed it so he couldn't keep quiet.

"Well I've been knowing about that." He said quietly. Elana stared at him wide-eyed due to shock. "You've known about what, all of it!" She exclaimed, Brian remained silent. "You too, I asked you not to lie to me Brian. You could of said something!" She yelled, she stood up but Brian raised up and grabbed her arm preventing her from leaving.

"It wasn't my place to Elana." He spoke softly and his voice had a hint of shame but most of it was pure regret. He felt terrible and wanted to say something but that's something a mother should discuss. "You never really opened up to me about your dad so until that night at the carnival I thought you already knew so I didn't want to bring it up if you didn't." Brian stated.

Her anger started to go away because she was seeing that Brian was making since. It wasn't on him to tell her how her father died and they did have a consistent relationship until he came back which was eight years later. She should be mad at everybody else, he just walked in on the situation. She looked in his eyes and saw that same look and there was no anger towards him, she smiled and gave him another kiss.

"How can I make it up to you?" He asked.

"There's one thing you can do." She said.

"Name it, and it's done." He said not expecting what she would ask.

"Talk to my brother about stopping this stupid war between Terell and Henry." She stated.

The thought of it made Brian want to laugh but he could see that Elana was serious about this which made him question her intelligence because he knew she was a smart girl.

"That situation is pass talking." Brian said as he shook his head and walked away from Elana amd around the bar as he grabbed a drink and a glass. The thought of doing that made him crave some alcohol. Elana followed him not giving up on her request.

"My brother said the same thing but he's willing to talk" She was consistent Brian thought and he didn't want them to go through with this anyway. If anything they both could learn a lesson about not being that greedy and sharing the territory.

"Elana, Terell is not gonna bend on this and you know him just as well as I do one of them are gonna have to die and I'm not directly involved in this like your brother is so you might want to be worried about him more than me." Brian said not realizing how cold-hearted that sounded but Elana did as she turned her back to Brian in disgust.

"So my brother doesn't mean anything to you?" She asked. Brian poured a shot into a glass and slurped it down quickly then filled up another one.

"Yeah, but not as much as Terell." Brian said walking over to her. "Giovanni is smart enough to take care of himself, you don't have to worry about him or me." He put his hands on her shoulders. "But I will talk to him if that will make you feel better." Brian said while he kissed the bottom of her neck. "I'll try to make him see that maybe we can put some kind of stop to this and find a truce option." He continued to kiss the bottom of her neck and got those butterflies going in her body.

She grabbed his arms and wrapped them around her and she felt safe in them. She knew she could count on Brian to help her. She remembered that feeling she had after talking to Giovanni. If Terell and Henry self-destruct and her boyfriend and brother make it out of this safe, she would feel better about the fact that she tried everything she could to stop the situation from happening

Brian and Giovanni both knew about the severity of this problem but were too loyal to leave Terell and Henry out to dry so they were making mistakes that could be fatal. They closed their eyes and hoped that everything would be okay.

Terell and Henry were on a collision course, Tommy and Tony were starting to become allies and a bunch of other small problems were brewing and it was all coming to the point where people were going to die all in the name of drugs, power, and money.

Mac stood outside of the spot smoking a blunt with his young friend Kevin. Kevin who admired Mac a lot a considered him his idol watched his mannerisms and mocked him. The relationship between the two were like father and son. But the age difference made them more like brothers which was the perfect blend as far as respect was concerned. Mac could teach him but Kevin was old enough to take Mac's words at the value he felt was beneficial to him instead of orders.

"These cats out here are going to constantly look at you as a target once you get in this game man." Mac said between drags of his weed. Kevin was hanging on to Mac's every word and soaking his wisdom like a sponge. "So when you show some kind of hustle it brings respect which can have two outcomes. Either they're going to hate it or love it and the real are going to love it. Can you dig that?" Mac said while he passed the blunt to his young but perceptive friend.

"Yeah, I can dig it." Kevin responded. The kid was a gangster in training but unlike Mac he was authentic. You could see the ruthless inbreeding but he had a heart. Not only from the compassion he had for his mother who was a drug addict but for the kids around him who were hungry. He would offer half of his food just to see his friends who were starving not go hungry.

"I've put blood, sweat and tears into getting money. Terell taught me some thangs but he's greedy for power not money and there's a difference. I'm greedy for money which means if it's beneficial we all can eat but Terell wants to make decisions. He thinks he's gotta call the shots in order to get paid which is backwards. That's why when the times right I'm taking over." Mac said with a smirk on his face. Kevin saw no wrong in Mac's blatant display of betrayal to his friend. In Kevin's eyes Terell would deserve what he got coming.

Mac heard the doorbell of the store ring and it was Ricky. He decided not to have Kevin around so he waited before he opened it. "Look Kevin, the lesson for today is over, you can take that weed with you but I got business. Get at me tomorrow." Kevin did as he was told and went out the back door, when he was gone Mac opened the door to let Ricky in.

"What took you so long to open the door?" Ricky said with authority in his voice. Mac was starting to get sick of Ricky and his attitude every since he put Ricky with Terell.

"Look man, I'm getting tired of you trying to tell me how fast I'm handling my business. Just because you getting tight with Terell don't mean a damn thing, I will slap the hell out of you, right here right now." Mac was starting to get careless because a statement like that could be interpreted as a few things but he didn't care.

"What do you mean, just because I'm getting in tight with Terell?" Ricky asked trying to catch on to the insinuation so he could tell Terell some more things about Mac to take away his trust.

Mac seen what he was trying to do and waived him off. He was starting to regret referring Ricky to Terell. He had no idea that he would be a consistent suck-up and praise Terell like he was some kind of God but he was seeing what Ricky was doing. He came to a conclusion that Ricky was trying to get in good with Terell and then snake him but he was going to beat him to the punch.

"It means be real man, when I heard about your rep, you sounded like somebody who wanted to be a boss eventually, not the man who was under the boss." Mac was trying to discredit Ricky's ambition in hopes to anger him so he would leave Mac alone, but that wasn't working out for him.

"I'm just playing my part which is what you should be doing. Terell runs the show and we can eat lovely off of him. I know that and you should know it to. He got the connect which means he got the muscle and if you can pull that trick and pay me more I'd be the same way with you." Ricky said coolly.

Mac took the time to think about what he just said and it was obvious that Ricky literally didn't have no ambition. There were some guys in the game who were content with being the muscle or second in command and he knew he needed a guy like that on his team. He decided that with some guidance Ricky could be a major asset when he tried to overthrow Terell and take over the game. But that conversation was for another time he was still putting together his plan to become one of the top kingpins and California and the more time went by the more Phil's proposition sounded good to him, with the right plan it would definitely work. In his mind all he had to do was keep Ricky off his back and Terell in the dark about his plans and he would be in great position to strike eventually.

"So what happened with that deal?" Ricky asked. Mac forgot about the lie he came up with and just gave Ricky a blank look which made him think that Mac was lying about it all. "The one you said you had with the Italian lined up, when we made that run with the Asians and I was waiting for you all day."

"Oh, he ain't got back to me yet, as a matter of fact I need to check up with him." Mac said sensing that Ricky was on him like a hawk, he knew that Ricky was running and telling Terell every little thing so if he was going to make his move it would have to be fast. "Look man the last think I need is the new guy coming in here telling me what to do." Mac said harshly. But it was too late Ricky was already on to Mac's game. He didn't know the full details but he knew Mac was up to something. He knew that Mac and Terell were going to clash but he didn't think Mac stood a chance so it was amusing to him to see Mac contesting Terell. But at the same time it would be beneficial because that would put him in Mac's old spot and unlike Mac he knew how to play his position and be grateful for the money and power he would receive in that position.

The tension between the two started to become evident and at one point Mac felt like he might of needed his gun but they both remained calm. Mac looked him as a servant and Ricky looked at Mac as a fool, either way Terell was in for a fight because there was one of his men gunning for his spot and the next one willing to see him go because he didn't feel complete loyalty to him.

"Is that all you came to talk to me about?" Mac asked.

"I'm just saying keep your loyalty man, if you ain't got the heart to be the boss don't try to be." Ricky was trying to initiate conflict so he could know who he would be under. He seen Mac's ambition but didn't believe he had the heart to be a real boss. As for Terell he seen that Terell's anger and ability to get caught in his emotions would mean his downfall. The two men both could be powerful if they would fix they're flaws but when it comes to being number one you have to have no flaws which is partly the reason Ricky preferred to be number two instead of the top man.

"Thanks for the warning man, now if that's it I got a few phone calls to make. You can sit in here if you think I'm trying some funny shit." Mac walked over to the phone but Ricky just stared at him.

"Nah, that's alright, I think I'll go see what's up at The Spot where my boss is and watch his back." Ricky felt like he got his point across but in return made himself look weak but it didn't matter to him. Only thing he was concerned about was collecting his money and not taking the blame when the heat would come down, besides Terell only hired him to watch his back and drive, not to show any kind of brains to run a successful drug conglomerate like the one that Tony built.

As Ricky walked out the room Mac made a phone call and some girl answered the phone.

"Let me speak to Phil." A couple of seconds went by and Phil was on the other end.

"Who is this?" He asked.

"Your new partner, so what's up with this plan you working on man, I'm in on it whatever it is, but we gotta move fast because I'm having a little problem on this end." Mac was ready to display the element of surprise Terell or nobody else would see this coming but it was.

"This ain't anything I can talk about on the phone, call me in a couple of days and we can discuss what I'm thinking okay." Phil stated as he smoked a cigarette and told his girlfriend to shut up. She was in the living room yelling at him for not taking the trash out. "Broads." Phil said calmly. "They want you to do everything for them but don't give nothin' in return."

"That's because you don't know what to do with them." Mac said like was a player, if he wasn't getting money he would have nothing but himself. Phil didn't respond to the last comment he just hung the phone up. Mac did the same thing and began to contemplate what Phil's plan was. He wanted to put it in action soon because he was running out of time.

Giovanni sat with his sister on his mother's couch questioning the decision he was making about talking to Brian. It was pointless in his eyes but whatever he could do to ease his sister's mind he would do it. There were a lot of rumors going around about Henry having a price on his head that had him worried. Henry was trying to be too ruthless and crazy stories were circulating that Giovanni didn't want to believe.

This one Russian dealer was fresh from Russia and set up a deal made by Phil. He was supposed to come pick up some kilos and take them back to Russia. He had the proper business manner and a reputation for being a stand up guy in the game. The only reason he was dealing with Henry was because of a recent drought that luckily didn't affect the Cartone family. Henry was known for having a sexist mentality and felt that women had no place in a man's business so when he met with the Russian he noticed that his partner was a woman. At first he a made sexist remarks to her which she brushed off because it was nothing she hadn't heard before. But when she wouldn't speak to him Henry got angry because it was a sign of disrespect she should have spoke when she was spoken to.

The Russian was getting irritated by Henry's distraction with his partner while business was being transacted. "Hey Cartone, let's do this business, huh. One time I deal with you and not again, maybe you need to grow up. I heard about your family's reputation and you're not upholding it very well." He said with a thick Russian accent. Henry felt himself burning up inside but left the situation alone because the Russian was right, they were there to make money so what if he wanted to have the inferior sex in with him that weakened his entourage` according to Henry.

Phil counted all the money in the money counter and it was a thousand dollars short. "You're short a Grand my friend." Said Phil with his arms crossed. The Russian put a wrinkle in his forehead and then looked at his female partner and said something in Russian. She nodded at the bag with the money in it and responded back in their native language. The male reached into the bag and grabbed a small stack of bills that was stuck in the cusp of the bag.

"Sorry for inconvinence but here it is." He handed Phil the money and Phil counted it by hand. "Were all set." Phil stated as he loaded the money up in a suitcase and closed it shut. Henry kept staring at the woman who was beginning to get annoyed by him.

"That's what happens when you have a bitch do a mans job." He said coldly.

"Grow a pair of balls then talk about being a man." She snapped back at Henry's remark and before she knew it he was grabbing her by the throat. The Russian man and his crew started to attack Henry but they were outnumbered with fully automatic weapons all pointed at them by Henry's team. They were out numbered men wise and over powered gun wise so the Russian had no choice but to watch his partner get the life choked out of her.

Henry was sweating and his face started to turn red along with hers, it felt good to him. He was releasing his anger on this woman who happened to come across a man who felt she should be home bearing kids not getting money. The fact that this woman had the audacity to be more paid then most of the men in his crew drove him insane. After her fighting went down she slowly but surely started to go limp and within moments she was officially strangled to death.

Henry let her lifeless body go and looked up at the man. "You can either take your stuff and go, or get killed here right now and we keep it, it's your choice." The man thought it was a dirty trick and would loose his money but he realized that Henry was no thief. He just had extreme opinions and when he was crossed he made sure the person crossing him paid the price which was the traits of a cold-hearted individual.

A knock at the door brought Giovanni out of his thoughts. Elana stood up and went to open the door. Once she opened it she hugged Brian before he walked in and seen Giovanni sitting on the couch.

"I'll be back later. You two try and listen to each other please." She walked out of the house and closed the door while Brian remained standing. Neither of the two men knew what to say to each other and neither wanted to start the conversation but both knew there was plenty to talk about.

"I told your sister that there was no point to us talking I don't want things to go down but I can't stop it." Brian said full of skepticism.

"You don't really have anything to worry about now do you. From what I hear you're not even involved in this, killers and drug dealers aren't coming for you." He said coldly.

Brian had no pity for him. Giovanni chose to get in the game and Brian kept out of it. Nobody made him make the choice to hop in this business with Henry but bringing that to Giovanni's attention made no sense and Brian knew that.

"Check this out man, Henry is doing too much and moving to fast. You need to talk to him I know you can't get him to leave the game alone but at least get him to chill out." Brian warned.

Giovanni seen through Brian's intimidation tactics but there was some truth to what he was saying. Giovanni wanted to see how much information Brian knew about Terell's plan. He was wondering if Terell was planning to hit Henry so he could warn his cousin.

"You sound like Terell got something up his sleeve already." Giovanni didn't want to probe too much but he had to be frank with him to get some information.

"I didn't say all that but Terell ain't gonna sit around while Henry make all these moves and not do something plus he thinks you guys were the ones that shot at him on the basketball court." Brian lied. He knew that Terell suspected Larry but he didn't know what Giovanni knew so he was playing the game correctly.

Giovanni didn't give Brian enough credit, he thought just because he wasn't involved in the game that he was stupid.

"So if it's a war then that's what it is but I'm not gonna tell you our next move." Giovanni was drawing a line he knew the conversation wasn't going as planned so he turned it into seeds of war. Brian didn't want to argue he was actually there to prevent one but he had to let him know where his dedication was.

"I'm trying to prevent it and I can tell that you are too. So why don't we both talk to them and try to get them to back up a littlie bit." Brian said. This is the kind of talk Giovanni expected would come from Brian and he was feeling the same way but he had to maintain the tough guy image so that Brian wouldn't think he was weak. He stared at him for a second pondering on a response. He felt that he needed to choose his words wisely and try to say something that could defuse the situation instead of making it look like he was giving in at the same time. The lines were drawn and unfortunately him and Brian were on opposite sides with his sister stuck in the middle.

"Even if I tried to talk to Henry, which I'm not even sure I want to do, he wouldn't listen to me." Brian believed him but for some reason thought Giovanni had the best chance to convince Henry to calm down just like he figured he had the best chances of getting Terell to do the same.

"Come on man, you know you don't want to be in the drug game. Like you said you're in this deeper than me but you don't want this life you just feel loyal to your cousin and there's nothing wrong with that. Just think about it, and see what you can do." Brian sat down, not to close to Giovanni but he wanted to put emphasis on his next words. "You could be the one to stop this cycle with our families and you're telling me that you don't want to. I don't believe that for a second, so just try and see what happens. At least you can know you made an attempt instead of doing nothing because at the rate those two are going somebody's gonna die." Brian stood to his feet and walked towards the door.

"Hey!" Giovanni called out. "If anybody's gonna die it's not gonna be me or anybody in family and you can tell Terell that." Brian turned around after Giovanni's comment with a feeling of hopelessness left in his mind. As he opened the door Elana came in.

"Where are you going?" She asked. Brian just shook his head as he walked out of the house. She turned to her brother.

"It's no use Elana, I tried and I told you it was pointless talking to him." Giovanni said as he stood up and walked into the kitchen to make a sandwich. Elana sat on the couch with her hands in her head quietly crying she had a bad feeling that something was going to happen.

⎯⎯⎯⎯⎯⎯

Gina got word to Tony quickly about Tommy wanting to meet with him. She felt that it was a shame that it took all this murder over the years for the two men to try and see things from the others point of view. The Cartone family never wanted to do business with blacks or make any moves in the black neighborhood. Tony was ambitious and Paul Cartone wasn't willing to deal with blacks to put him on so it was a war brewing. Now they realize that there is no money in a war and they are dealing with their sons going at each other. Terell was walking around looking at his father as soft. He thought there was something going on between him and Gina which would have been disrespectful to his Uncle Jimmy. Jimmy was dead but there was some lines you didn't cross and being with your brother's woman was one of them.

Tony sat in his favorite chair in his bar as usual drinking his brandy and smoking a cigarette. Terell came down the stairs with more footsteps following him. They belonged to Ricky and Mac and the three men sounded like a military coming. Tony listened to them walk through the living room and enter the bar area. Terell and his crew surrounded Tony which gave him a slight feeling of a ambush. He knew nothing was going to happen to him physically but he could tell another argument with his son was in the makings.

"Is there something you gotta say to me?" He asked Terell with irritation in his voice. Tony was about to lift his son out of his shoes if he kept up his insinuations that his father had gone soft. Tony knew the real and he loved his son so he let a lot ride that he wouldn't of taken from nobody else.

"I'm planning to hit Henry Cartone in a couple of days and I just want to let you know." Terell said coolly, he had his mind made up and he knew what his father was going to say to him. Tony could try and talk him out of it until he turned blue in the face but he was tired of waiting. "My money is slowing up, he disrespecting the game he giving California dealers a bad name. Somebody gotta do something about him, plus I hear he's trying to get at me." Terell was lying through his teeth but he ran out of things to say to get his father on board for what he wanted to do to Henry. To him, if hearing that Terell knew that Henry was going to take his life didn't spark some fire under his dad then there was no point call him dad.

"You know what, I'm working on wiping out everybody with Tommy Cartone. Fuck his son, you do what you want but I'm trying to finish my war I can't worry about yours." Tony said as he stood up and turned his back on his son for the first time in his life. He had a shot of brandy in his hand and he drunk it.

"Pop, why are you letting that bitch trick you man?" Terell questioned with his hands in the air.

"You are ignorant. You can't listen, I gave you all the knowledge about this game and you just throw it away. Maybe I made a mistake letting you take over my business and giving you my connections. Maybe I made a mistake retiring, you might not be ready." Terell folded his arms as he listened to his father. "I made my decision though, I'm legit, I do legit things, and I'm fine with that. I don't have as much money as I used to but I do good for myself. Your problem son is not hustling, it's communicating. You don't have the tolerance of a kingpin, you got that street mentality which will hurt you in the end." Tony walked back over to the bar and poured a shot.

"Yo Terell, let's roll man." Mac said. He was amused by Tony and his lack of aggression.

"What is your plan son if you have one." Tony asked, he didn't think Terell had enough smarts to even have thought that far ahead. He was learning a lot about Terell through this experience and he had lost faith in his ability to run a business, let alone stay a alive with all these sharks in the water hunting for his spot, a spot that he was handed and didn't earn at that.

"Come on man don't play me. I know what I'm doing. Honestly I don't really want to tell you, it might get back to Henry some how." Terell said, he was joking but the comment angered his father. "I'm gonna meet up with Ricky and Mac then hit his spot, he found out about my spot in back of the Asian store but he don't know I moved it. We are gonna light that shit up and I don't give a fuck about who's in there. Elana ain't gonna be there so nobody else matters." Terell smiled at his father proud of himself for his plan.

"What about your other cousin?" Tony asked finding a flaw in Terell's idea.

"He's on the enemy side and he'd do the same thing to me." Terell noticed that his father was shocked about his strategy to hit Henry even though he didn't agree with the move. It made Terell happy because his father wouldn't admit it but the pride for his son was glowing. The fact that Terell found out where Henry's spot was made him respect his son and he had enough sense to make the move from his spot was one of the smartest decisions he made.

Tony watched his maturity but wish he would of listened to him instead of going against his wisdom. He also looked at Mac and thought how Mac was a bad right hand man. No drug kingpin could be a good one if he kept soldiers around him that weren't cut out to be upper echelon military minds.

"I'm begging you son, wait a day or two before you do this. Once I handle this problem I got were gonna sit down with you and Henry and discuss a solution because after I make this move it's gonna be right. We can do what we should of done ten years ago." Tony said as he drunk his shot and was heading to the bar to get another one as well as he lit up a cigarette.

"You ain't gonna redo your mistakes through me man, the sooner you see that the better off we can be. I'm not waiting on shit. I'm gonna make the move tonight now, instead of a couple of days we doing it tonight!" Terell yelled.

"Come on man, let's go." Mac said. Terell stared his father down for a second before him and his crew exited. Tony stood speechless as he shook his head and drunk his liquor. He inhaled his cigarette harshly and blew the smoke out.

"Very young and very stupid." He whispered to himself, he couldn't worry about Terell he was too busy finishing up his own demons and finishing his own battle. He wondered if he could trust Tommy Cartone. He felt he could but to him the only way to really know was to look the man in his eyes.

Henry was watching Scarface with a plate of coke in front of him. Giovanni sat next to him watching the movie uninterested. It wasn't that he didn't like the movie he was tired of it. That movie had every gangster in America watching it hundreds of times. Henry watched intently with his eyes wide from cocaine. He did another line and handed Giovanni the plate with a one hundred dollar bill rolled up on it. Giovanni took it and fixed himself a line.

Henry sat back and flicked his nose as he remained mesmerized by the movie. "Look at this spick the whole world was his and he ruined it up by shooting somebody over a women and some kids. If it's a job it's a job to me. Bada bing, bada boom they would have been dead." Henry spat, his words made Giovanni sick. He hated what his cousin was becoming, he was out of control.

Giovanni's mind started racing as he did the two lines unwillingly. He hated cocaine and the way it made him feel but peer pressure was something that he gave in to. He started to think about what Brian said. If anybody could get through to Henry it was him and he believed that with plenty reason to. They had been tight since they came out the womb even before Jimmy died. It was something that drew him more to Henry then Terell even though they were all the same age.

"What's on your mind cousin, your being too quiet over there. Is it Sonny? Are you still mad about that?" Henry did feel some remorse for it but it had to be done he was paranoid about Sonny trying to take him out when it was really Phil. The only one he never worried about was Giovanni.

"Nah Henry, honestly I never like the prick anyway." Giovanni answered handing Henry the plate back. Henry laughed as he fixed himself two more lines of cocaine.

"You might think I'm too wild sometimes and that I'm out my mind but I know what I'm doing and I'm not gonna create any situation that I can't handle. I just need to know your with me because if your not just get out now." Henry sniffed the powder quickly and made two more lines. "I know you got balls because you've been in it this long. If you got any second thoughts let me know because somebody is gonna try and hit us. I don't know who it is but it's somebody. It might even be your cousin." Henry sniffed the lines harshly again and passed Giovanni the plate.

"Come on man, you know I don't even talk to him. But I did talk to Brian." Henry gave him a blank stare. "Elana's boyfriend, the one that was at the carnival and he had a good point." Henry sighed he wanted this conversation to happened but he didn't think it would. He started to feel betrayed by Giovanni but he had no reason too so he studied Giovanni's face. His cousin better choose his next words right if he wanted to remain on Henry's good side. On top of that Henry was high he would never kill him but he would smack him around pretty good if he said anything to Brian that jeopardized them or they're business. "We should all walk away from this war and come up with an agreement to share the territory." Henry started laughing, he thought his cousin was joking and had him all nervous for nothing. Giovanni fixed himself a line and sniffed it as Henry grabbed the plate. He was still chuckling as he carefully maneuvered the razor he was using. His nose was red and running, you could tell he'd been doing a lot of coke recently.

"You almost had me going, you mean that kid actually thinks it's still a chance to be reasonable. He's even more dumb then I thought. Terell's planning something I know it and when he does, we'll be ready." Henry said between sniffs.

"Look I'm with you cousin all the way to the end but this is getting out of hand it's like I can see my death date." Giovanni put his head in his hands and for the first time ever Henry could sense the fear in Giovanni over loosing his life. His cousin had been doing a great job of pretending for him, so he could feel like he had somebody to trust. Giovanni was risking his life for Henry and nothing that anybody could say or do would ever mean more to him. But at the same time Giovanni had to buck up, he made the decision now he must ride it out. Henry put the plate on the table.

"Look Vanni, I hope you made the right choice by being close to me. You know death is a good possibility in this business but were making money and that's what it's about. That's the big question. Forget me, is the money worth you loosing your life one day. Don't be scared." Henry picked the plate back up and continued watching the movie Giovanni just watched him. "I don't want to think that your black side is untrustworthy cousin I know our blood can overpower that. But, your dad was a doctor for Christ sakes and he still couldn't be trusted, so I hope you ain't the same way." Henry was blatantly testing him, he never spoke to him like that and Giovanni started to notice a change in him. He didn't know if it was the money or the power, or maybe all the coke Henry was doing but he had to make a change in his life. Brian's words were hitting him harder now more than ever. Get out the game while you can he thought.

Mac and Ricky were parked in front of the same river that the Carnival was at. They were waiting on Terell so they could hit Henry's spot. It had a different feeling now. Long gone were that lights and energy now it was more of a quiet calm tone. You could hear the water and crickets. The cold vibe was evident. Mac watched as a car rolled up and parked, it wasn't Terell it was Phil. Mac watched as he turned the light off and became incognito. His black Lincoln matched the night time and it was damn near impossible for Ricky to see it. Mac's aim was to get rid of Terell and he thought about killing Ricky but wasn't sure. He was going to kill Terell and offer Ricky a proposition to work for him, especially after the last conversation they had.

Phil was under the impression that they were going to knock both of them off and then go kill Henry in the same night. Henry had just got his new spot and neglected to tell Phil about it. After the situation with Sonny, Phil kept his distance which made Henry wonder about him. The plan was for Phil to not be seen until he spotted Terell and to drive up and start shooting.

Mac watched Ricky as he smoked his cigarette, it was obvious he was either nervous or anxious. "Don't get scared nigga!" Mac exclaimed. Ricky gave him a look like he lost his mind. He wasn't scared of nothing but he was in deep thought. He didn't trust Mac as far as he could throw him and it was strange why Terell was taking so long to show up.

"What the fuck is taking this nigga so long man, we might miss Cartone all together." Ricky said angrily, he hated when things didn't go as planned. If you weren't going to follow through with it why plan it was one of his philosophies. He had no problem going at a situation all wild and just busting heads but he wanted to do things the right way and this situation wasn't even organized. They were supposed to wait a couple of days but instead they did it off a whim due to Terell's anger. When the plan changed Mac had to get word to Phil about the new plan through Kevin.

Terell's car pulled up and he turned the engine off. "There he go man you can stop bitchin' now." Mac spat as he lit up a cigarette and Terell got out of the car. His eyes were low because he had smoked a couple of joints in the car. He didn't do coke but he smoked a lot of weed in his lifetime. His demeanor was calm as he watched his crew and anticipated a move he had been ready to make for a long time.

"What's up yall?" He said addressing his comrades. Are you ready to handle this, we ain't leaving nobody out, everybody in there dying." His words were sharp as he looked at his crew like a coach preparing his basketball team for one last run in the fourth quarter of a championship game.

He started clapping his hands and seen that Ricky was his usual rigid self with no expression verbally but his face said all Terell needed to know but there was something off about Mac and it startled him. He stared down Mac who lit up a cigarette avoiding eye contact with Terell.

"What's up Mac you don't like what I'm saying or do you got something else on your mind?" Terell asked as he studied his best friend and all in one second the snake in Mac started to rattle Terell's brain. It's like he could smell and sense all Mac's plotting and deception all at once. "Mac, what's up man?" Terell asked again this time his eyes were wide open.

"Nah boss. I'm with you." Mac responded coolly as he looked up at Phil's car parked behind them. Terell followed his eyes but he didn't see the car. It was dark and plus Terell was high so his eye sight wasn't one hundred percent. "I'm just following you." Mac gave him a smirk but it was forced and Terell noticed. Every second that passed made Terell feel like grabbing his gun and shooting his closest homeboy but it was something holding him back. He knew that Mac had something to hide but he wasn't ready to give up and see him for what he really was, a backstabber. Ricky saw it, Tony seen it, but in some weird sense Terell wanted to believe Mac was down for him because that was who he choose for years to have around him.

"Let's go Terell before they leave." Ricky said with urgency his mind was on killing and he couldn't wait to get business handled. He was hoping Henry had some money in the spot so they could get paid before they took his product and hustled some money.

"Okay, let's do this!" Terell said and the moment they turned around to walk to the car, Phil's lights turned on and he sped over to them shooting. The three started shooting shots but Terell moved quickly into the dark so Mac couldn't get a shot off on him. He was trying to avoid Phil because he was unaware that Mac was aiming for him also. Phil crashed into Terell's car and opened his driver door to use it as a shield.

His window was rolled down so he started shooting while he was knelt down behind his door. Everybody started shooting except for Mac who was on the side of Ricky. He seen Ricky's body drop as Phil caught him with three shots. Terell was shooting at Phil while Mac was aiming at Terell. He couldn't get a clean shot because Terell was behind a tree so he started shooting wildly at Phil, intentionally missing him.

Phil felt bullets coming from Mac's direction and felt double crossed, so his anger rose and started firing shots at Mac who duck and retreated behind a tree. Terell noticed the heat off of him and on Mac and ran from behind the tree and crept to the other side of Phil's car.

Phil's adrenaline was rushing at this point and he was screaming as he let off the rest of his clip at Mac. Luckily Mac came out of the situation with no bullet making contact with his body.

Terell heard that Phil was out of bullets so he made his move around the car while Phil was putting a new clip into his gun. As soon as he finished loading it he felt Terell's barrel on the top of his head and seconds later he couldn't feel or hear nothing but death. His body dropped and Mac came from behind the tree and walked over to the two men, one dead and one alive.

"Your aim was off Mac." Terell said sternly, he stood up and walked over towards Ricky shaking his head. "This nigga was a soldier, damn Rick." He watched as Ricky laid with his eyes open. Terell bent over and closed them then stood back up. He had love for Ricky and never thought that he would be gone like this. He envisioned a life long partnership with him like his dad had with Eric.

"Come on man, are we still hitting Cartone or what?" Mac asked, just because Phil was dead his plan was still in full swing, he would just have to figure out how to get Terell too.

"Nah man, not tonight, come help me get him to the doctor so we can burry my nigga right man." Terell said sadly.

"He gone T, but we need to worry about your car first this white boy smashed it up!" Mac exclaimed. He walked over to Terell as they picked up Ricky's lifeless body and put it in the backseat. They walked over to the driver and passenger seat of the car got in. Terell's car started and he backed up with his front in ran in from Phil's car and drove off leaving Phil dead on the scene.

Tony and Gina drove to the gates of the Cartone mansion and he still couldn't believe that he was about to have a face to face meeting with Tommy Cartone the son of his sworn enemy for all these years. That was more surprising than being in the same car as the wife of his dead brother and daughter of his sworn enemy. But things change and the rules to life get twisted and bended in the drug business. Lives had been lost and new enemies who were on the same side had been formed and unlikely partnerships have came together in this last year. Gina had become involved in something she wouldn't of been involved in if Jimmy was alive. Since his death she had become a different woman. Her decisions were less pure and more for revenge, it was like when she lost Jimmy she lost her innocence.

Tony marveled at the mansion, it was the first time he seen it. He never planned to live in that manner, he could have but his house was humble just like he was. He was impressed and remained silent when he got stares from Cartone's henchmen who guarded the house. They all knew who Tony was and most of them had shot at him or survived an altercation with him, or have had fallen soldiers because of his hands and they weren't too happy to see him and have orders not to touch him. Tony looked at them with smiles because he knew it was burning them up.

Tony parked his car. They stepped out and walked to the steps of the mansion. For a split second

Tony had a feeling he might have been set-up by Gina and ambushed but it didn't last very long. They walked in the doors and down a long corridor to a small intimate part of the house where the fire place was. It was a wide hallway with a couch placed against the wall opposite of the fireplace. The glow of Tommy's face and the shadow of the fire was visible to Tony on the wall. Gina sat down next to her brother who had a glass a wine in his hand and kissed his cheek. Tommy was a boss now, a retired one but a boss nevertheless.

"Have a seat." Tommy said as he raised his eyes up at him. Tony was already staring at him so it was the first time that they actually made eye contact. Both men felt an admiration for each other but that cautious mind to attack still loomed. It was surreal for Tony because he felt like he was getting ready to make a deal with the devil but he wanted to hear what it was.

Tony remained silent and kept watching Tommy as he anticipated a move. "You're still the cowboy you once were I see. Before I say another word, I need to hear it from you, swear on the lives of your children that you didn't kill my father." Tommy watched him and waited for a response, if Tony just swore he would believe him, but if Tony started giving explanations then he wouldn't.

"I swear of the lives of my sons that I didn't kill Paul. Neither did my son." Tony was embarrassed that he couldn't keep Terell under control but Tommy had a similar problem with Henry so he didn't feel any weaker by releasing that information to him.

"That's a problem for a later time that we need to deal with but for right now I think we should team up and focus on this issue at hand. Delena is trying to wipe all of us out. He's using my father's brother to turn on me." Tommy shook his head because the thought of his uncle's betrayal still hurt his soul.

"I don't know if he's mixed up with Carlo Delena but my bodyguard is planning something, and the only thing that would give him the balls to do that is having somebody to have his back maybe with the pull that Delena has. I know that Delena doesn't want to run my part of town, and Leroy is the closest man to me so that leads me to believe maybe Leroy made a deal for my son's territory." Tony said as he kept thinking about any other things that might need to be addressed about the situation. "We gotta hit them, I don't know exactly what they're waiting for but we gotta figure out what are Leroy and your uncle doing for Delena and my guess is taking us out." Tony expressed knowing that Tommy already knew that.

"But when is the question. I think he's trying to get my kid too but I would think I'm first on his list. He won't come here because he knows it's a fortress. But what's stopping him from coming to your house to hit you?" Tommy asked. Tony thought about it before it came to him.

"They're planning to hit us together." He said confidently.

"But that wouldn't make any sense because they know we don't be around each other and I haven't even left the house and I don't plan to until my nieces, well our nieces, graduation." Tommy forgot for a second that she was Tony's niece also and as a sign of respect he corrected himself.

"She's my niece too, and Brian is my son so he's graduating also, Leroy knows that." That was all they needed to figure out to have the upper hand. The decision to link up was already starting to benefit, it was two warlords who were on their game to destroy their enemy. It made sense Leroy's plan was to hit them both at the graduation.

"Now all we gotta do is figure out when to hit them which should be right before the graduation, and I can find out the time to do it." Tommy was more better to formulate the plan to get in because he knew the Delena family inside and out. "The graduation is in two days and that means we should hit him the night before, we need to figure out a way to get in."

"I want to be a part of this Tommy." Gina said anxiously, she seen that Tony and her brother were on the same page and she wanted to be included.

"I don't know Gina." Tommy didn't want to get his sister involved but he could sense that she wasn't gonna take no for an answer. "Ok, I'll figure out something for you to do." He said.

"What information can you give me about the inside of the house?" Tony asked. Tommy started to remember what his father said about Delena. He liked his privacy at night, he hated having a lot of people in his home and his security cameras were put there to watch his house. So he only had Carman on guard, who he always had around and his wife in his house at night. He just put a lot of men outside of his house to watch the perimeters. Tommy shared this information with Tony who found it very useful.

"Delena is married but Carman always orders a girl, you know, pays for sex. Maybe we can find a girl for him." Tommy said. Tony got déjà vu. Him and Tommy literally planned things out the same he remembered how he got Larry killed with the same strategy.

"Actually that's where we can use Gina." Tony said, he received sharp glares from Tommy and Gina

"Tony that's sick, I'm not having sex with that man!" Gina exclaimed.

"Come on now, you think I would do that to you. Listen all you got to do is find out which one he calls, get a time so we know when. If it's just him and Carlo alone, Tommy can make calls to the unions and get some kind of layout of his property then we can do this." Tommy was impressed, and his ego was elevated that this man who can plan so well could never hit him.

"We sure did have some wars though." Tommy didn't think that a friendship between the two men had blossomed but they weren't enemies which was a large improvement in their relationship.

Gina noticed this and felt some sort of relief but seeing the two of them made her think of Terell and Henry and she hated to see this war recycle.

"What about the boys?" she asked. This day for Tony made him realize he wanted to do this hit and then that was it, Tommy felt the same way.

"I don't know about you but I'm too old for another war." Tony said shaking his head.

"So we let them handle their own affairs?" Tommy asked.

"That sounds good to me." Tony said with his hand extended, Tommy shook it and it was settled, the father's had let they're sons go along with the drug business. They just wanted to get these traitors off their backs and then go on and live peaceful lives. They knew they're sons weren't going to last in this game, they were too greedy and power hungry. If they didn't kill each other one of the sharks out there would do it and that was just the truth.

Terell sat on a king size bed in a plush hotel room while Brian was scrambling around it getting it ready for Elana. He was so excited about this night and it wasn't just about the sex. Brian and Elana were about to consummate their love for each other and make it as real as it could be. Brian was adjusting the lights and he had a bottle of champagne in a bucket of ice. He grabbed a bag of handpicked rose petals and looked over and saw that Terell had now laid on the bed and got extremely comfortable.

"Get up man." Brian said sternly. Terell heard his tone of voice got up and laughed at Brian.

"You are going all out over some pussy" He said between laughs. "Maybe Mac was right you are a sucka for a woman. She got you like this before the sex just imagine how it's gonna be for you after." He started to shake his head. "I'm gonna hate to see you tomorrow bro." Terell stood up as Brian started putting the petals on the bed.

"See, you wouldn't know nothing about this because you've never had a woman that was worthy of this type of treatment. So I don't expect you to understand." Brian said still focused on his night and not Terell's words. He finished with the petals and threw the bag away in the garbage.

A booming knock came at door and he heard the words room service follow it. He opened it and a cart of delicious food from the hotel came rolling in. The servant looked around and smiled noticing Brian's skills at being romantic. Brian moved the cart by the bed and looked up at Terell.

"Drop him a twenty for me bro, I don't have change." Brian asked.

"Now you giving me orders, you better calm down a little man." Terell snapped jokingly as he gave the man a twenty. The servant spun around and walked out of the door then shut it behind him. "I can't believe Ricky's gone man. Through all this shit he's been a soldier, now he's dead man." Terell didn't know Ricky that long but it was something that made him feel like Rick was going to always be loyal to him and satisfied with his position. "Last night though, it was something about Mac that made me feel like he's a snake. He had a look and just after is when some Italian ran on us shooting. Remember when Ricky was saying that Mac had a meeting with some Italian?"

"Yeah." Brian responded half way paying attention because he was setting the plates up.

"I just thought about it, the white boy we killed was Italian and he might be a part of Cartone's crew." Terell said solemnly. He was convinced that Mac was a traitor and it pissed him off that he let his ego get in the way of Ricky's life and his judgment. "I've been looking for him all day and he hasn't been seen, I should of seen it and been killed him a long time ago." Terell had a personal pint of Gin in his pocket he pulled it out and took a couple of swigs before putting the top on and placing it back in his pocket. "I'm gonna get him." He said to himself.

Brian noticed how drunk he was and walked up to him and gave him a hug. "Look man, it's gonna be alright, if you need me just let me know." He assured Terell that he had his back, and Terell knew that he meant it. Brian knew Terell had nobody by his side so if he wanted to he would accompany him on his quest to hit Henry. But Terell would never allow that, it just made him feel better to know that he had his back like that.

"I'm gonna go smoke Henry Cartone after your graduation, he's on the low right now from what I hear and he still don't know I moved my spot, so I'm going alone to finish this, don't worry about me." He said patting Brian on his back and standing to his feet. "Enjoy your night." He said as he walked to the door and opened it. He looked back at Brian who was crushing the ice with the champagne bottle, he smiled and closed the door behind him.

Brian took a minute to grab some champagne glasses from under the table that the champagne was placed on when he heard a soft knock on the door. He rushed to it and took a deep breath before he opened it. He saw his angel standing on the other side and his knees got weak as she walked in wearing a stunning red dress that was tight fitting and came down to the middle of her thighs. She looked around and then back and Brian and nodded her head obviously impressed. He had went all out and this was how she imagined loosing her virginity, in a setting like this.

As soon as she walked in the room had a vibrant feel to it. In Brian's head was up and down, one minute he would hear Congo drums and wild animal noises, next it was violin strings and shade' music. His mind was all over the place but his body was calm and smooth.

"What are we eating?" She asked sitting down at the table in front the food, the tops were on the plates. She really wasn't hungry but it was all part of the night. Brian opened the champagne and let the suds hit the floor as the cork popped. He filled both glasses up and then started to prepare a toast, as he raised his glass Elana followed suit.

"To us, forever." Brian said smoothly. They both drunk the champagne swiftly the taste was delicious as Elana shook her glass indicating that she wanted more and Brian poured both of them another glass as they ate they're meal. It wasn't a lot of conversation just stares of love and smiles. They were doing more drinking than talking but Elana wasn't doing as much as Brian because she really didn't drink. Brian was used to Brandy so the champagne wasn't strong enough to have him drunk.

After the meal and courtesy mint Elana stood up and walked over to the bed touching the rose pedals which reminded her why she felt that Brian was the one for her, he knew the right way to do things with her, to make her react the way he wanted, and she didn't mind giving a man that type of control because in a way it still gave her control over herself.

She took her heels of and laid down on the bed and removed one of the straps that held her dress up and then the other, she lowered the dress showing her bra. Brian walked over to the bed and laid down on his side kicking his shoes off and kissing her shoulder. She lowered her head back as his tongue swerved around to the bottom of her chin, then to the bottom of her neck. His hand went up her dress lifting it till it was scrounged at the mid section of her body. He grabbed it from the top and removed it down her legs and off her feet she was stunning in her bra and panties. Her flat stomach with her round ass and perky breast made his eyes widen and heart flutter. He was in awe of this woman physically and emotionally.

Elana laid him on his back and sat on his groin area and removed her bra, her breast didn't move a second and her nipples were almost as round as nickels. Brian removed his shirt rolled over and took his pants and underwear off while he did this she took her panties off and the two bodies collided in lust mixed with love behind it. Brian broke her cherry and the painful pleasure filled Elana's body. She didn't want him to stop when he asked her. Brian felt her insides and treated them gentle until she got used to it. He loved watching her face experience the pleasure and pain of having her virginity taken. They weren't married but he knew that she was the one he would spend the rest of his life with.

Brian rolled her body over and she wrapped her legs around him she was picking up on the rhythm pretty quickly and he could see she was a natural her eyes were locked on his and it was to the point where the vagina wasn't too tight that it cut off the circulation of his manhood. Her moans turned into soft cries and tears streamed down her face but she was in ecstasy and loving every minute of it. Brian never experienced passion, lust, and love at the same time and he felt himself climbing to the peak. The experience was going past the half hour mark and Elana didn't want it to end, Brian had to slow his rhythm down in order to make sure she got the full experience. He started to feel her moans getting louder and her grasp on him tightening and that's when he knew she was almost there.

With his climax not far behind he went into hyper drive giving her swift a long strokes as she started to raise the level of her enjoyment in her voice. Moments later the two both reached the mountain top and Elana was screaming as she felt her first orgasm. They both felt like they were in heaven and it was perfect, the whole night, it was like they were soul mates and they just realized it and found each other. Elana turned over and looked at Brian before laying her head on his chest and not another word was spoken. The two went to sleep with no care in the world.

Brian was always nervous when he went to his grandmother's house because she was so adamant about how she hated Tony and he wasn't her grandchild for referring to him as his dad. Even though Marvin abused Brian for years it never dawned on her how the abuse was, she just called it a child getting spanked by their parents and there was nothing wrong with that. The only reason he was going over to the house that day was to give her a graduation ticket along with his mother who came into town.

Brian walked passed a couple of strung out junkies on the corner and walked passed an alleyway where a girl was performing oral sex on a drug dealer. Brian hated seeing those images but he wasn't in the part of town where he lived, he was in one of the roughest part of Los Angeles which was South Central. He approached the house with the tickets in hand wishing he could drop them off and leave, and not even talk to the women. It might have been harsh but that's how he felt. He loved both women to death but the more they defended Marvin for what he did to him the less he wanted to be around them. For years his mom was talking down Tony for what he did to Marvin but nobody seemed to discuss what Marvin did to him.

Brian knocked on the door and his mom opened it to let him in, she hugged her son tightly and kissed him on the cheek.

"How's my baby boy?" She asked with a huge grin on her face.

"I'm good mom, I got the graduation tickets for you and grandma." He said as he walked into the house and through the living room. His grandmother was standing in the kitchen looking out of her window. "I brought you a ticket for my graduation." He said softly. She kept looking through the window.

"This is the first time you've been here since you've been back for a year and you expect me to go to your graduation. I'll go but I'm mad at you grandchild." She responded without looking at Brian.

Brian's mom walked into the kitchen and opened the refrigerator door and grabbed a pitcher filled with lemonade she poured a glass sat at the table and lit a cigarette up.

"So what's that no good man up to these days, is he with that white girl yet. His brother's wife." She asked angrily. The question irritated Brian, and he had to hold his tongue.

"Mom Tony wouldn't do that to his brother even though Jimmy's been dead for nine years." Brian said trying to get her to stop bad talking Tony and ruining his good mood.

"Trust me son. I know if Tony wanted a woman he would do whatever he could to get her, don't let that man trick you." She snapped. "Do you got a girlfriend out here?" She asked switching her tone to a more happier one.

"I'm actually with Elana, Jimmy's daughter." Brian stated.

Brenda spit her lemonade and dropped her cigarette on the floor. Her reaction caught Brian off guard but he remained silent waiting for some kind of explanation why she flipped out about him going out with Elana. She narrowed her stare at Brian as she picked her cigarette up and puffed it, she took another sip of her lemonade and took a deep breath.

"I remember Jimmy Taylor, he was a doctor and a good man, not like his brother." Brian's grandmother said still looking out of the window.

"Have you slept with her Brian." Brenda asked nearly crying. That's what made her so mad Brian thought, he forgot that his mom must of thought he was still a virgin. So he didn't want to make matters worse on her and let her continue thinking that was virgin.

"No mom, I haven't had sex with her." He said coolly, but he still was bothered by her reaction.

"Thank God, leave her alone Brian, whatever you do don't be with that girl." She expressed while she shook her head and smoked her cigarette. Brian was tired of people trying to get in the way of him and what he wanted, but he wasn't going to get into it with his mother because he wouldn't be seeing her that much now that he was going to school out here and she still lived in Atlanta so he was just going to ask why then leave it alone, because he was so curious.

"Why mom, what's the problem?" He asked.

"That's Tony's niece, you can't have nothing to do with her like that, just be friends or something. You can't be with no girl related to Tony, he's not right." Her request sounded more like a plea than an order which made him more curious but he decided to leave it alone. He set the graduation tickets on the table.

"Mom I don't know where all this hatred for Tony is coming from but I don't want to hear it, to me that's my father, not Marvin. No matter how much you wanted me to look at him like that I don't, sorry grandma." Brian knew his words about her son would hurt her feelings but that was a sore subject for him and she knew that. It was a silence and it seemed very uncomfortable.

"I slept with him Brian." Brenda said in a low voice, it was almost a whisper.

"Who?" Brian asked blind sided by the statement.

"Tony, before your father I was having sex with Tony, and Marvin knew about this and still perused me. I didn't love Tony though, I ended up falling in love with your father and Tony hated me for that, he never got over me all these years later. Do you think the reason he killed Marvin was because of you? You were only an excuse for him to justify killing Marvin for me not choosing to be with him." Brenda took one last drag of her cigarette before ashing it in the ash tray that set next to her right elbow. She grabbed another one and lit it up staring at her son waiting for an reaction.

Brian noticed his mother was chain smoking and she only did that when she was nervous which made him believe there was more to what she was saying. He couldn't see Tony killing his best friend over a female and the thought of it was too much for him. But one thing was certain this is something he had to ask Tony immediately.

"I love you both but I got to go, I hope to see you tomorrow." Brian walked over to his mom and gave her a kiss on her head, then walked to his grandmother and for the first time he'd been there she turned away from the window and gave him a kiss on his cheek, he did the same and walked out of the house and back into the concrete jungle. Something about that visit rubbed him the wrong way but he didn't care he was in love and ready to get to the next part of his life. Why would his mom be that mad about him with Elana? Did her hatred for Tony run that deep to the point where she want any aspect of him cut out of his life? That was it he thought. She always said Terell would be dead in a couple of years anyway and he was going off to college so if he got involved with Elana then he would still have some sort of connection to Tony.

His mom was going to be disappointed because he was as committed to her as ever. She was the love of his life and in time Brenda was going to have to accept that he was having sex and it was with Elana. She's going to have to learn how to live with the fact that he loves that woman, and nothing was going to change that, he thought to himself.

Terell walked into the living room of the house and seen that Tony was hanging up the phone. He was pacing around smoking a cigarette and had a unopened bottle of Brandy on his table. He never drunk in the living room it was always in his bar and Terell watched as his father was definitely in deep thought. He watched Tony for a second and didn't want to argue with him so he started to walk out the door, Tony finally recognized the fact that there somebody in the room with him and snapped out of his thoughts.

"Where you going son?" Terell stopped midway stride through the front door and turned back around. He didn't want to tell him to avoid an argument.

"Out to The Spot." He said monotone. Tony knew about Ricky getting killed and seen that he wasn't with Mac so he put two and two together, either he was going to look for Mac or Henry Cartone.

"Which one are you going after?" He hoped his son would listen to him because he got the strangest feeling that this would be his last time asking him. Tony agreed to let his son make his own decisions but considered this his last chance to get it through his head to leave his anger be just for the moment. "I'm not going to tell you what to do, I'm not going to try and stop you from what you want to do. All I ask is that you think very carefully about what your next move is."

"You know what Tony, that sounds more like a threat than a request." Terell said coldly.

"I didn't hear you son, what did you call me?" Tony asked wide eyed. He couldn't believe his ears. Everything he had done for that kid and this is the amount of disrespect he shows him. Tony rose to his feet and walked up so close to Terell that he could small the Gin on his breath. He had been in the same clothes since yesterday and Tony could see the rage in his eyes.

"I called you Tony, because a father is gonna be on a son's side no matter what." Terell spoke sharply and felt a little nervous he knew his father's strength and knew that he couldn't beat him up but he didn't care, he was staring eye to eye with the man that gave him life and he didn't respect him for that.

"A father will teach a son and guide him, but when the son don't want to listen and think he knows everything, then that's when it's time to let him stand on his own two, and that's what I'm doing." Tony said still debating if he was going to lift Terell off his feet or not.

They stared each other down and for a second Terell didn't look so tough. It look like he was getting to the point where he was going to break down and ask for help and before Tony could embrace his son or reach out to him the phone rang. Tony knew it was either Tommy or Gina and he had to answer it but he felt like he needed to be there for his son. After the third ring Tony went to answer it.

"Hello." He spoke low. "Okay I'll be there, it's still the same plan right? Alright then." He hung up the phone. When his eyes met Terell's that wall had been put right back up and that slim hope had gone. Terell knew what that was about and he knew it had something to do with the Cartone family. He wasn't one hundred percent positive but he knew. He walked out of the door without saying another word and Tony didn't try to stop him he walked to the door to watch him walk down the driveway.

He lit up a cigarette and went back to thinking and watched the time go by. The seconds were moving by slow and after ten minutes he heard his front door open and seen Brian standing there staring at him. The look on Brian's face threw him for a loop at first he thought Brian might have wanted to punch him but after further examination it was like he was just looking for answers.

"What's on your mind? Please no more drama I just went through that with your brother." Tony pleaded. He took a shot out of his glass, and noticed that Brian was still staring at him. "Okay son, what is it, what did I do to you?" He wasn't in the mode for an argument and he was confused on what Brian could be mad at him about anyway.

"It's not what you've done to me, but to my mom years ago." Brian responded in a calm but yet stern tone. "She tells me that you two had something going on before Marvin, then she choose him over you."

Tony turned his head straight and poured another shot. He chuckled to himself. Brian was getting impatient, he wanted Tony to give him an explanation.

"That's how she said it happen, she's not all the way wrong but she didn't tell you why she chose Marvin. She had no choice but to, I wouldn't be with her because of the life that I was living. On top of the fact that Terell's mom was the real love of my life. That's why I told her that we couldn't be together." Tony didn't want to get into the discussion anymore but he knew Brian was going to keep at him for information especially since Tony said his mom wasn't being all the way truthful with him.

"Why didn't you tell me?" He asked.

"Because it wasn't a big thing, your mom didn't want me to say anything to you, and Marvin knew it was before him so I guess we all put it in the back of our minds." Tony's mind had too much on it for him to be dragging up these memories with Brian so he stood up with his bottle and grabbed his keys to leave and take care of the situation at hand. Brian seen what he was trying to do and decided to pull out the most important question that he had.

"Is she the reason why you killed Marvin? She said you were jealous of him so you shot him and made me think that it was about me." Tony stopped and set his keys down, he turned around with a look of evil in his face. The nerve of Brian to ask him that sent his control flying out the room. He was close to putting hands on Terell and contained himself but not this time.

Tony ran up on Brian and grabbed him by his neck and shook him viscously. Brian's face turned red and for about ten seconds on non-breathing he could feel himself starting to get faint and almost passing out. Tony realized the severity of his chokehold and let go.

Brian dropped to the ground gasping for air and looking up at Tony with shock in his eyes. That was the first time Tony ever put hands on him and Tony immediately felt regret. He want over to Brian and reached out his hand to help him up. Brian just kept rubbing his neck and rose to his feet by himself.

"For one, I would never be jealous over a bitch! Do you know how many bitches I could have at the snap of my fingers, the answer is plenty. Two I hated that muthafucka for what he did to you, period! and since I took a father from you, I felt it was my job to replace him for you. But if you want to believe a woman scorn that's on you, I'm not going to let you or Terell worry me anymore. Your brother doesn't listen to me at all and now you bring this bullshit to me. I got shit to do I'll see you at your graduation." Tony walked over to the table and grabbed his keys.

"I dropped the tickets when you choke the hell out of me. They're over there on the floor." Brian said. Tony walked over to them and picked them up he sat them on the table where his keys were.

"I will be there tomorrow." He said as he walked out the door.

Carlo Delena sat in his home with his bodyguard Carman and like Tommy Cartone told Tony there were no men in the house with them besides his wife who was upstairs in they're bedroom. Carlo was happy about the events that he felt were unstoppable and nothing but beneficial for his family. He planned on having the whole state under his control and do nothing but sit on his fat behind and count money. He would have people doing all the work and the police wouldn't know that his family was still in the drug game. As long as Leroy and Charlie handled their business he was set.

Carman had already made his order to a female escort service and he was waiting for the girl to show up while waiting for the word from the boss that he could go retire to his bedroom. Carman was a skilled killer but his request from Delena to be at his becking call prevented him from having his own life which included women so Carlo personally handled his bill for escorts and tonight would be one of those nights that Carman happened to make his request.

"What is taking them so long, it seems like that moley has Charlie running on his time now." Carlo sneered. Carman showed a slight smile as he continued to reading his magazine. He had his mind on the pretty young woman that should be knocking on the door any second.

The doorbell rang and Carman went to go answer it still reading his magazine. He opened the door and didn't even have to look up to see it was Charlie and Leroy. He kept his gaze on the reading material and walked back to where Carlo was. Charlie and Leroy followed him.

"Hey, it's the only Cartone that I ever liked tell me you got good news for me Charlie." Carlo said excitedly. Charlie walked in and kissed Carlo on each of his cheeks with a smile on his face. Leroy remained standing because he still didn't know how to act in front of a man as powerful as Carlo Delena.

"Everything is according to plan Carlo, we got the snipers, the whole place is scouted, it's a shame that a terrible thing has to happen at a good celebration." The four men start laughing.

"Hey Leroy, how does it feel to be the first black guy in the home of Carlo Delena." Carlo said. Leroy thought he was joking but he was seriously staring at him waiting for an answer. Leroy wanted to tell him where he could go with that question but instead gave him the sensible response.

"It's an honor Mr. Delena and I hope to be here again soon when we do business."

"Definitely, but I shouldn't have to tell you what happens when people let me down right, in anyway?" Carlo asked. This time he had a different look on his face still serious but this one was more deadly. Leroy understood what Carlo was saying which was under any circumstances if he felt it necessary he will kill him and everything he loved.

"Let's toast gentleman! Carman grab us some wine." Carlo exclaimed. As Carman followed his orders the doorbell rang again and he knew it was his girl. He hurried back to Carlo, Charlie and Leroy with only three glasses then set them in front of Carlo and whispered in his ear.

"Go ahead, a man's gotta do what a man's gotta do, I guess." Carlo said with a smile on his face then proceeded to grabs his glass. Charlie and Leroy followed suit as Carman left the room and went to go answer the door. As the door swung open to his surprise it wasn't just one girl but two.

The first one was looking in his face with a smile and the second one was standing with her back to him. Noticing his confusion the first girl wanted to clear it up for him.

"Since you're a very loyal customer we thought we give you a little special tonight, two for the price of one." As she finished her sentence the second girl turned around and it was Gina. Carman's eyes popped out of his head. He had never seen Gina but she was just his type. He had attractions to all types and normally ordered different types of women but there nothing like a full bread Sicilian and he could tell she was one.

Carman got so excited that he forgot to check the women and let them in the house which was how Tommy hoped his plan would go. He walked in and directed them upstairs and followed them with an extra bounce in his step.

Carlo was in the middle of one of his drunken lectures that he liked to give especially to people he just met and he was letting his guard down. It was one thing to do business with black people but another when you were a boss of his age to have him them in his house. Some mob families didn't see color especially in the late 1970's, but Carlo was an old school mob boss, he didn't allow them in his family but he was getting older and it was the eighties. The bottom line is that he wanted the territory that the blacks were in but didn't want to be in it. Even slave masters had their house negro that they tolerated.

"You gotta be smart when your in any kind of business, and that's how you last. I got all this from these." He put his drink down and held up his stubby paws. He picked his drink back up went back to rambling.

Tommy and Tony crept through the backyard of the mansion and seen an opening the led down to an open door that Tommy paid one of Carlo's men to prop open. As they approached the staircase that led to the open door a henchman came form behind them. They just missed him and went down the staircase. The henchman stopped for a second looked around then kept making his moves watching the grounds.

They crept in the house with they're guns out and found themselves in a basement that had been turned into what looked like the back of a restaurant. It had freezers and big stoves all around with huge amounts of pots and pans hanging up. They snuck through the area and slowly came to a corridor with another staircase to the left. Tommy led the way as Tony followed him both men remained silent and were light on their feet.

Gina watched Carman and the call girl kiss on his bed and his eyes were locked on Gina's while his lips were on the call girl's. Just his stare made her stomach turn. She had a gun in her bra strap and was waiting for the moment she could use it on him. Tommy told her to hold him off for as long as possible but if he laid a hand on her then shoot him dead.

The call girl started taking off her clothes which got his attention, she stood up so she could give him a glimpse of her whole body and he like what he saw. She started moving her body to a rhythm and even though there was no music it was still seductive.

"What's she here for doll, she's just suppose to sit there and look pretty, what kind of two for one is that." Carman barked. He wasn't the finesse type, he wanted what he paid for and he was about to let the beast out of the cage. Gina thought about the gun right then but thought twice about it.

"Shut the fuck up!" She shouted. "I do, what I do, when I want to, I'm extra, you didn't pay for this." Her accent was thick when she got mad and that turned Carman on, his face went from angry to aroused. He couldn't believe how she could achieve that by just yelling at him. It was some type of euphoric feeling going through his body.

The call girl got up and tried to hug Carman but he pushed her to the side, his interest in her was gone he already had his eyes on what he wanted. He took two steps forward then stopped, he tilted his head to one side then the other and examined her frame.

"Okay doll, I can play your game." He said. The way Carman was focused on only her gave her chills and she was running out of tricks.

"Tell me you'll do anything I say." She ordered.

"I'll do anything you say." He responded.

"Lay on your back!" She yelled.

With no hesitation Carman hopped back on his bed with his legs laying straight forward and his arms to his side with his tongue hanging out of his mouth like a dog.

Carlo was still talking to Charlie and Leroy when his wife came to the top of the stairs.

"Carlo are you coming to bed?" She called.

"In a minute, I'm talking here." He yelled back. "Where was I, oh yeah, it was 1945 and I had just made my mark as the boss. I got the okay to start my own family out here. Some crazy guy wacks a boss, it was one of the rare times wacking a boss wasn't planned you know. You remember that, right Charlie?" Before Charlie could answer his question he went on. "So I did what I had to do and I've been on top for years, now when you get into this thing you gotta be careful. Hey nigger! I mean Leroy, I'm sorry I need to show you some respect were working together, but I'm not used to it you know." Carlo stated. "But do you understand what I mean Leroy, you gotta be careful, my name can't be spoken, not to anybody." Carlo was drunk but Leroy seen he was focused and knew what he was saying it might of sounded like drunk talk but it wasn't.

"Yeah I hear you Mr. Delena, where's your bathroom at?" Leroy asked.

"It's down that hall to your left." He answered, then resumed talking to Charlie as Leroy headed in the direction where the bathroom was located.

Tommy and Tony came up the staircase and poked they're heads around the corner to find a long hallway that went to the living room, from there Tommy could hear Carlo talking and Charlie laughing and he could also see the back of what looked like Charlie's jacket. His blood boiled it's one thing to know in your mind that somebody is a traitor, but when it's confirmed that's even worse. He leaned back and whispered to Tony.

"There in there come on." Before they moved they heard a door open and stepped back then they went a few steps back down into the dark and waited until they saw Leroy pass and walk into the living room. "All three of them are here, just our luck come on." Tommy whispered.

The two of them crept back up the stairs and walked into the hallway that led into the living room. When they stepped foot into the living room they were still un-noticed.

"They'll never know what hit 'em" Carlo said laughing.

"Nah fat man, you don't know what's 'bout to hit you." Tony said.

Tommy and Tony had their guns pointed at Carlo, Charlie and Leroy and they were caught in a position where they couldn't do anything and that's when Carlo started to look around at Charlie and Leroy with drunk angry eyes.

"You set me up, didn't you. I should of known better to trust a nigger and a Cartone! Carman! Carman!" He yelled at the top of his lungs, then he started to cough harshly until Tommy shot him several times to his death. His body slumped to the side but he didn't roll off the couch. Charlie and Leroy stared up at the two men they really tried to set-up, they could care less about Delena's false accusations.

Gina was standing over Carman with one knee on the bed he was slapping his hand on the bed hard motioning for her to get something started, she was feeling like she couldn't hold him off any longer so she was about to pull the gun out until Carman heard Delena screaming for him.

"Carman stood up and ran pass Gina to the door and turned the door knob. Gina grabbed the gun from her bra and a pillow to muffle the sound and fired two shots into his back. As he turned around she fired two more into him before his body hit the floor.

The call girl shivered in the fetal position because it was the first time she seen a dead body. That was the first time Gina killed a man but for some reason she didn't panic or fall apart. She rushed over to the call girl and comforted her for a second before grabbing the girl's clothes and getting her to come out of her state of shell shock. She stood her up and shoved the clothes in her hand.

"Come on, it's happening just like we planned, in a minute you'll have enough money to get you and your son out of here, you just gotta stay with me." The girl nodded her head as she started to get dressed, Gina waited for her as she looked out of the door to see if anybody was coming. She gave Carman another look and his eyes were wide open.

Tommy walked close to Charlie with the gun on him and never broke eye contact as he was going to enjoy this murder more than any other one he ever did. Charlie was searching for someway to get out of it but he couldn't come up with one, he thought about Tony.

"Look Tommy, I was trying to get Carlo of our back, he didn't kill Paul that cowboy did, don't let this meeting confuse you." Charlie could see it wasn't working so he tried to get Leroy in with him. "Ask Leroy here, he was just following Tony's instructions, they hit Paul ask him." Charlie was scared out of his mind, he knew death was creeping and he was handling it like a coward. Leroy on the other hand was acting like a man. He stared at Tony with a careless look on his face.

"What's up Leroy, you gonna tell me some bullshit too, or what?" He asked calmly.

"No I wanted the whole hood for myself and the fact that you gave it all to your son and not me pissed me off so I got an opportunity and I took it." Leroy said accepting his death, Tony nodded his head, raised his gun to Leroy and shot him in his face before he walked over to him and shot him until his clip was empty. He kept pulling the trigger even when the gun started clicking.

"You see how he just killed him Charlie." Tommy started. "I wonna kill you ten times worse. You were my father's brother and you switched on us when we needed you the most." He pistol whipped Charlie and Charlie tried to get up and run but Tommy shot him in the leg and knocked him back to the floor. Charlie crawled as Gina and the call girl came down the stairs and stopped once they seen what was going on.

"For all I know you could of killed my father!" He shot him again in the back, Charlie winced in pain. "Don't scream or I'll make this very slow." Tommy threatened. Charlie turned around to look at his nephew. "Tommy please!" He begged. "Don't do this, were family."

"Say it Charlie, tell the truth did you kill my father or have him killed. You're gonna be dead anyway just tell me." Tommy was crying at this point and Charlie seen the emotion in his face, he knew he was dead so he did the only thing he could do which was admit to killing his brother himself.

After hearing the words Tommy shot Charlie in the face once and then dropped his gun. Tony stared at him and then at Gina who was also crying.

"Okay I know this was emotional but we still got all these people outside we gotta get by they might be coming in soon so we gotta move. Gina you and baby girl meet us where we met and Tommy were gonna go back the way we came in. Revenge has been dished now we can get on with our lives." Tony stated with the only clear mind in the room. Gina and Tommy were hurting from this revelation from their dead uncle and the call girl was shocked she got caught up in this mess. This part of the family war was over but there was still unsettled business between the Cartones and the Taylors. With all the silencers used and the faint shot from Gina's gun Cartone's wife stayed upstairs through it all and was the only person who wasn't killed inside that home.

————————

Brian stood on stage as he was ready to accept his diploma and he didn't really feel anything. Things were as crazy in his personal life that this big moment didn't seem so big. He tried to be happy for himself, because all the work he put in finally paid off and he was one step away from his goal, but it didn't seem that important. His mother and Tony had been hiding a big secret from him for all he knew Tony could have been his father if his mom had got pregnant and she just could of wanted Marvin to be his father which would of made Elana his cousin. He got shivers just thinking about that but that was not the case because Tony wouldn't even let anything go down between them two knowing it could of been a possibility. Also, his mother didn't know they were having sex and if she knew they were seeing each other she would of definitely told him that Tony could be his father to really keep him away from Elana which would be the only thing that could.

He looked over at his woman and smiled at her, she wasn't letting anything ruin her day. Even though she was done with school and knew she was going to be in the entertainment business she was happy she achieved her diploma. The principle started calling the names of the kids and they would get applauses from the people they invited. Everybody was there from the neighborhood that Tony lived in. Gina, Giovanni and Tommy were there. Brenda and Brian's Grandmother were there. Tony was there and Brian could see off in the back of everybody was Terell watching him with a pint in his hand drinking.

Brian couldn't see his brother but he knew that Terell had that same smile he always had because he was proud of him. Terell hadn't been himself since Ricky died. He was obsessed with catching up with Mac who made an escape and hadn't returned since that whole altercation took place.

As the principle kept running through the names Brian seen Tony walk over to Tommy and Gina and automatically went to being alarmed, he wasn't aware of the truce between the two men so he was expecting sparks to fly. He didn't know what to do so he just watched as the two men were standing next to each other talking. He noticed that Tony was listening to Tommy Cartone and when he finished speaking they shook hands.

Brian was amazed. It was like a breath of fresh air that made him assume everything was alright and the war was over. These two were the ones who hated each other and if they can make some kind of step towards working things out they must have sat Terell and Henry down and got things settled. Maybe that's where Tony rushed off to last night thought Brian. He looked at Elana again but he couldn't tell if she saw what he was seeing. Then he heard her named being called.

"Elana Marie Taylor." The principle announced. Her supporters cheered her on as she went and accepted her diploma. She walked across the stage with one hand on her hip and the diploma in the other. She sat down with the rest of her class, and waved to Brian.

Brian was waiting for what seemed to be like forever for his name to be called and when he walked across the stage to receive his diploma he watched all the happy faces and proud looks that he received from all of his supporters that came to see him graduate. He thought about the people in the crowd who had love for him and how he was ready to move on with the next phase of his life. He thought about how his life would be with Elana and how she would be trying to get her career started in modeling while he would be going to school, the thoughts racing through his mind had him excited.

Tony and Terell both had graduation presents for him and he knew it was money. Money is one thing he never had to worry about but he didn't want handouts all the time. He wanted to get to a point where he didn't need it but college life was expensive even with a full ride scholarship and he didn't want to struggle, especially when he didn't have to.

After the ceremony he found his woman and hugged her tightly, she was smiling from ear to ear and it made his heart fill up with joy to see her so happy. Terell came up behind her and put his arms around her nearly scaring her out of her skin. She jumped and noticed it was him and hugged him.

"Congratulations girl, I'm proud of you." Terell said happily, she hugged him again. "You better make me proud whatever you do."

Elana may not of approved with a lot of Terells decisions but she did have love for her cousin. She knew he had a good heart but it was buried under a lot of pain and vengeance, along with hatred and that just comes with the territory of being raised as a gangster. He let her go and stared Brian down. His eyes told it all, there was a look in them like he felt content. He knew Brian had much more potential than a high school diploma, but it was the start of something great for him.

They embraced and if Brian wasn't mistaking he might have thought Terell dropped a tear but he was mistaking. He felt a strange vibe coming from his brother and contemplated on weather he knew something about what just happened between Tommy Cartone and Tony when he was on stage.

"I just seen Tommy Cartone and pops shaking hands does that mean the problems are over and this situation is done." Brian asked.

Terell stared at him for a moment. "Stay out of this Brian, you just worry about your day man. Get on that bus and go on your senior trip." Terell spoke quietly and then stared off into the distance, he saw Giovanni getting in his car to leave and then looked back at Brian. "I'm gonna handle this today." He said a little more sternly but still calm.

"Wait, what is going on?" Brian asked as Terell walked off, Brian grabbed his arm.

"Don't do this Brian." He warned.

"What, your gonna knock me out?" Brian pushed, he was testing Terell who thought about it for a second then he remembered who he was talking to and how smart Brian was. He knew Brian was trying to get him to put his mind on Brian's antics and off the bigger picture so he just snatched his arm out of Brian's grasp and walked off. "Watch your back man!" Brian yelled hoping Terell would hear him, he seen Terell raise his arm up indicating that he did.

"Come on Brian we need to get on the bus before we get left." Elana stated. She seen that Brian wasn't responding so she stood in front of him. "Let's go!" she insisted.

"Go on without me." He said coldly, he wasn't going, and his mind was made up. Elana instantly got worried that he was going to get involved in the family drama.

"No Brian were going now!" She exclaimed trying her best to get him to come with her. He just stared at her surprised that she had the audacity to try to give him orders. He walked off and followed Terell taking off his cap and gown but holding on to his diploma as he went to his car.

Mac watched Terell get in his car and Brian get in his and waited for both of them to pull off, so he could follow them. He knew where they were going or at least he had a feeling where and he had the drop on everybody because as far as they knew he was long gone from California anyway, well at least to Terell who was looking for him.

Henry was getting a drop off ready at his dope spot with a cigarette hanging from his lip. He looked ragged from a long coke run he had previously been on. This fast life had been wearing Henry down and he was in a spiral. His reign would eventually come to an end before it really began and it was a sad case. The grandson of a drug genius is what the mob would say, it would dishonor the Cartone name. The Cartone family were good about being kept out of the mouths of the law and the feds were starting to hear things. But Henry didn't give a fuck about that and with Tommy getting out of the drug game he didn't care too much about it either. He was legit and a greater legitimate business man than drug dealer.

Giovanni came into the spot and Henry picked up the gun next to him and pointed it at Giovanni in an extreme case of paranoia. "Jesus Christ cousin I almost blew your head off." Henry exclaimed.

"Sorry maybe I should announce myself when I come in." He slowly lowered his hands. "Are you okay Henry." He questioned seeing his cousin's appearance and noticing how he could literally heard the drags Henry was taking of his cigarette due to the harshness he was hitting it with.

Henry finished getting the packages ready and zipped the bag holding the contents shut and threw both of them on his shoulders, he was looking around for his car keys.

"I'll be doing better once we get this money. We got to meet this mick by the docks, are you ready?" Giovanni nodded his head and looked like he wanted to say something but before he could get a word in he felt a barrel to the back of his head.

Giovanni stiffened up as Terell slowly pushed him in the room with the gun to his head. Henry pointed his gun at Terell.

"We got a crazy situation here. One cousin is trying to save another cousin from getting his head blown off by his cousin. Is that funny to anybody but me." Terell was intoxicated but he could see that Henry was high, he liked his odds with his aim over Henry's.

"Drop the gun!" Henry screamed, "I will shoot your black ass." Terell thought he might but with him having Giovanni put Henry in a compromising position.

Brian pulled up outside of the spot and seen Terell's car he wasn't going to go inside without a gun so he looked in his glove compartment and grabbed one.

"What the hell am I doing." He said in a low tone. He never shot a gun before and here he was going into a gun fight. Something in him wouldn't let him walk away from it. He opened the door and slowly walked up on the building. Just like clockwork Mac rolled up and parked out of distance. He had his gun in his lap already loaded. He opened the door and got out. Once he spotted Brian he chuckled to himself.

"This cat must be dumb or he finally got some heart. This is gonna be like taking candy from a baby." He started walking cockily down to the spot following Brian at a distance. He showed no respect for him because he wasn't trying to be careful at all. He could careless if Brian saw him, the way Mac looked at, it was too late for Brian to grow a pair of balls now, so whatever he was doing didn't impress him.

Giovanni elbowed Terell in the stomach and ran to the other side of the room by Henry. Terell backed around the corner he came around with his gun still out. He had the wall to protect him but lost his edge on Henry. He didn't panic but felt like he had to think of something fast before the two would kill him. Giovanni pulled his gun out and the two slowly started to creep to the wall.

They knew Terell still had the drop because they didn't want to come around the corner and get shot before they could turn at the right angle. They maneuvered slowly to check and see where he was at.

Terell started to retreat, he couldn't believe he let that cousin of his pull a fast one on him which made him have to revise his strategy but he wasn't done. As he got to the door he bumped in to Brian who was behind him, he turned around and almost shot him. Brian jumped and Terell noticed who he was and pulled him to the side looking at him astonished.

"What are you doing here man?" He said turning back around to see if they were coming. He grabbed Brian and ran to the side of his car knowing that Henry and Giovanni were about to come out of the door. Tony grabbed the gun that Brian had. "Give me this and get in your car then when you see them come out, try to hit them. Go now!" Brian did as he was told and Terell had both guns pointed at the door.

Brian opened the door and started his car soon as Giovanni and Henry came out. He was parked backwards to the door so he drove in reverse to try and hit them. They moved out the way, Giovanni diving to the ground safely and Henry jumping off balance in the open. As his body flailed around in the air as Terell shot him three times, catching him with every bullet.

Brian stopped the car and as soon as Giovanni stood up, he heard a shot. Giovanni ducked down behind Brian's car as he heard more shots in the opposite direction. He looked off at the area that he heard the shots coming from and seen Mac shooting Terell down. He shot in their direction not to try and save Terell from Mac but because he saw enemies.

Mac got in Terell's car and drove off. Brian backed up and opened the door for Giovanni who got in and instantly pointed a gun at Brian.

"What are you doing?" Brian asked in a panic.

"About to blow your head off!" Giovanni exclaimed.

"For what?" He responded.

"You just tried to hit me with this car!" He yelled. Brian focused on keeping pace with Mac and Giovanni finally lowered the gun from his head. He thought about Henry and tears came to his eyes. Brian seen what Mac did to Terell and all he could think about was seeing him get what he deserved. He wasn't no killer but he knew only a coward would shoot a man in his back and that's what Mac was.

Giovanni watched as Brian was keeping pace with Mac, he wasn't sure if it was Terell or Mac that shot Henry, Brian wasn't either but Giovanni wasn't letting Mac get away. He watched intently and silence filled the air in the car as neither one knew what was going to happen next.

They gave chase through parts of the city on their way to the train station in Los Angeles and once Mac reached the destination he parked Terell's car and hopped out. He left his gun in his car so he could get pass security. Seconds later Giovanni and Brian were parking and getting out the car also. Giovanni put his gun in his pants and walked in with Brian closely behind him.

The station was crowded and Mac went to get a ticket he was going to go get out of town for a minute and then comeback. Once word got around about what happened like it does, his name would be solidified as boss material. He waited in the line checking his watch waiting to get his ticket, and it was finally his turn to order one.

"Round trip to Sacramento." He said. The young girl went into her computer. She was new so it was taking her a little time to get his request set up. "Hurry up." He snapped. The girl looked up angrily but the sadistic look on his face, along with her customer respect kept her from yelling back at Mac. She kept doing her job and printed his ticket out, he snatched it from her and started walking towards the gate to get on his train.

Giovanni and Brian kept looking through the crowd for him and Giovanni spotted Mac standing by the train. He didn't say a word to Brian, he focused on Mac and walked towards him with his hand on the end of the gun sticking out of his pants. Mac didn't see Giovanni coming and didn't look in his direction at all.

As Giovanni approached him Brian wanted to call his name out and tell him not to do what he was thinking because killing Mac right now would put him in jail for life. But his lips couldn't move fast enough he watched as it look like Giovanni was moving in slow motion. Giovanni was pulling the gun out and shooting Mac dead from about ten feet away.

The crowd disperse and security was all on the situation. Giovanni didn't try to run or fight he dropped to his knees and locked his hands behind his head and then turned around and looked at Brian.

"Take care of my sister." He said, but Brian couldn't hear him or read his lips. He motioned his head to tell Brian to get out of there and Brian slowly backed away. The cops and security approached him and started to do their job. He stared at Mac's lifeless body on the ground and had no remorse. The cops read him his rights and he gave nothing but non-verbal communication. They picked him up and walked out while Brian watched the whole time not knowing what to think he was just happy to be alive and away from all this.

The way he was thinking at the graduation started to make since, this tragedy had to happen, and he had to experience it to fully understand that he had to dedicate his life to change what has happened around him growing up, even if he didn't succeed it's what he had to do.

After Giovanni was taking all the way out of the train station Brian followed them outside and walked to his car. He caught one more eye contact moment with him before he was shoved in the cop car Brian got in his car and drove off, it had been a long year and he was glad to be moving on.

Tony and Gina stood in the front yard of his house watching Elana and Brian load up his car to get on the road. They weren't going too far and with a half a million dollars from father and son they were set. Also money would be there from Elana's family. They weren't even going that far just to USC, and it felt like they were leaving a whole completely different lifestyle. It was a new beginning for everybody and they hoped that euphoric feeling would last forever.

Brian wasn't aware of what he was going to do but he knew he was going to be a writer in some way. His major was journalism but he was trying to understand himself as a person before he could focus on how to express himself as a writer but that was the journey he embarked on with the love of his life by his side he was ready for the task.

Elana was ready to jump in the spotlight and be seen. She wanted to be a model, actress, singer, dancer, and be known for then just as a beautiful girl who tuned into a gorgeous woman. All she was missing was the glamour and that is what she was intending to happen. She had Brian there to support her that's all she needed to start the next chapter in her life.

Tony was retired from the drug game trying to figure out what was next. He thought of a few avenues but nothing stuck out to him, he had to eat. He saved a lot of money over the years but he needed something to do. He was thirty-eight years old and already lost a son. He was proud of Brian and knew he would make something out of himself, and in the back of his mind Marvin almost messed that up with the way he treated Brian.

Gina hugged her daughter and Tony hugged his son, then they hugged the other person and set to leave. Henry, Terell or Giovanni wasn't brought up. Terell and Henry were dead and Giovanni was going to be incarcerated for Mac's murder. It was a tough time but the two of them were the stars that shined bright amongst the clouds of despair that filled up the lives of these two families.

Brian and Elana said their final goodbyes and got in the car and drove off. Brian looked in the rearview and saw waves from the two and then he focused his eyes on the road and looked over at his woman who was deep in thought and happy which made him smile too.

When the sight of Brian's car was gone tony turned and looked at Gina. She looked back at him and for the first time ever Tony seen a look that he thought he would never see and it was love. She wanted him, and he could tell, he tried to resist it, he tried to look away but she kept the stare on him and started hypnotizing him. Next she positioned her body directly in front of his and put her hand to touch his face.

He wrapped his arms around her hips and pulled her close to him to where their mid-sections were smashed together and they kissed. It was a passionate kiss as the wind blew in Gina's hair. Tony felt regrets even though his brother had been dead for years and he didn't have any feelings for her until now, he felt wrong but he didn't care she had him wrapped.

A car was parked from across the street and the occupant was watching them. It was a woman and she kept a close eye on the two. She shook her head and started the car up. Brenda pulled out of her parking spot and drove off and past the two with a blank look on her face. She seen now that Gina was in her way to get what she wanted, but Brenda knew she would get what she wanted.